This book is for Devin

ROGER ZELAZNY
CHANGELING

Illustrated by Esteban Maroto

CHANGELING

CHANGELING

I.

When he saw old Mor limp to the van of the besiegers' main party, the Lord of Rondoval realized that his reign was about over.

The day was fading fast behind storm clouds, a steady drizzle of cold rain descended and the thunder rolled nearer with each beat, with each dazzling stroke of light. But Det Morson, there on the main balcony of the Keep of Rondoval, was not yet ready to withdraw. He patted his face with his black scarf and ran a hand through his hair—frost-white and sparkling now, save for the wide black band that passed from his forehead to the nape of his neck.

He withdrew the finely wrought scepter from his sash and held it with both hands, slightly above eye-level, at arm's distance before him. He breathed deeply and spoke softly. The dragon-shaped birthmark on the inside of his right wrist throbbed.

Below, a line of light crossed the path of the attackers, and flames grew upward from it to wave before them. The men fell back, but the centaur archers stood their ground and unleashed a flight of arrows in his direction. Det laughed as the winds beat them aside. He sang his battle-song to the scepter, and on the ground, in the air and under the earth, his griffins, basilisks, demons and dragons prepared themselves for the final assault.

Yet, old Mor had raised his staff and the flames were already falling. Det shook his head, reflecting on the waste of talent.

Det raised his voice and the ground shuddered. Basilisks emerged from their lairs and moved to stare upon his enemies. Harpies dove at them, screaming and defecating, their claws slashing. Werewolves moved in upon their flanks. On the cliffs high above, the dragons heard him and spread their wings . . .

But, as the flames died and the harpies were pierced by the centaurs' shafts, as the basilisks—bathed in the pure light which now

shone from Mor's staff—rolled over and died, eyes tightly shut,
as the dragons—the most intelligent of all—took their time in descending from the heights and then avoided a direct confrontation
with the horde, which was even now resuming its advance, Det
knew that the tide had turned, his vultures had come home to
roost and history had surprised him in the outhouse, so to speak.
There was no way to employ his powers for deliverance with old
Mor out there monitoring every magical avenue of egress; and as
for Rondoval's physical exits, they were already blocked by the
beseigers.

He shook his head and lowered the scepter. There would be no
parlaying, no opportunity for an honorable surrender—or even
one of the other kind. It was his blood that they wanted, and he
had a sudden premonition of acute anemia.

With a final curse and a last glance at the attackers, he withdrew from the balcony. There was still a little time in which to
put a few affairs into order and to prepare for the final moment.
He dismissed the notion of cheating his enemies by means of suicide. Too effete for his tastes. Better to take a few of them along
with him.

He shook the rain from his cloak and hurried down the hallway. He would meet them on the ground floor.

The thunder sounded almost directly overhead now. There
were bright flashes beyond every window that he passed.

Lady Lydia of Rondoval, dark hair undone behind her, turned
the corner and saw the shadow slide into the doorway niche. Ut-
tering a general banishing spell, appropriate to most unhuman
wights likely to be wandering these halls, she made her way up
the corridor.

As she passed the opening, she glanced within and realized immediately why the spell had been somewhat less than efficacious.
She confronted Mouseglove the thief—a small, dark man, clad in
blackcloth and leather—whom she had, until that moment,
thought safely confined to a cell beneath the castle. He regained
his composure quickly and bowed, smiling.

"Charmed," he said, "to meet m'lady in passage."

"How did you get out?" she asked.

"With difficulty," he replied. "They make tricky locks in these parts."

She sighed, clutching her small parcel more closely.

"It appears," she said, "that you have managed the feat just in time for it to prove your undoing. Our enemies are already battering at the main gate. They may even be through it by now."

"So that is what the noise is all about," he said. "In that case, could you direct me to the nearest secret escape passage?"

"I fear that they have all been blocked."

"Pity," he said. "Would it then be impolite of me to inquire whence you are hastening with— Ah! Ah!"

He clutched at his burned fingertips, immediately following an arcane gesture on the Lady Lydia's part when he had reached toward the bundle she bore.

"I am heading for a tower," she stated, "with the hope that I can summon a dragon to bear me away—if there still be any about. They do not take well to strangers, however, so I fear there is nothing for you there. I— I am sorry."

He smiled and nodded.

"Go," he said. "Hurry! I can take care of myself. I always have."

She nodded, he bowed, and she hurried on. Sucking his fingers, Mouseglove turned back in the direction from which he had just come, his plan already formed. He, too, would have to hurry.

As Lydia neared the end of the corridor, the castle began to shake. As she mounted the stair, the window on the landing above her shattered and the rain poured in. As she reached the second floor and moved toward the winding stairway to the tower, an enormous clap of thunder deafened her to the ominous creaking noise within the walls. But, had she heard it, she might still have ventured there.

Partway up the stair, she felt the tower begin to sway. She hesitated. Cracks appeared in the wall. Dust and mortar fell about her. The stairway began to tilt . . .

Tearing her cloak from her shoulders, she wrapped it about her bundle as she turned and rushed back in the direction from which she had come.

The angle of the stair declined, and now she could hear a roaring, grating sound all about her. Ahead, a portion of the ceiling gave way and water rushed in. Beyond that, she could see the entranceway sliding slowly upwards. Without hesitation, she drew back the bundle and cast it through the opening.

The world gave way beneath her.

As the forces of Jared Klaithe pounded into the main hall at Rondoval over the bodies of its dark defenders, the lord Det emerged from a side passage, a drawn bow in his hands. He released an arrow which passed through Jared's armor, breastbone and heart, in that order, dropping him in his tracks. Then he cast the bow aside and drew his scepter from his sash. He waved it in a slow circle above his head and the invaders felt an invisible force pushing them back.

One figure moved forward. It was, of course, Mor. His illuminated staff turned like a bright wheel in his hands.

"Your loyalty is misplaced, old man," Det remarked. "This is not your fight."

"It has become so," Mor replied. "You have tipped the Balance."

"Bah! The Balance was tipped thousands of years ago," said the other, "in the proper direction."

Mor shook his head. The staff spun faster and faster before him, and he no longer appeared to be holding it.

"I fear the reaction you may already have provoked," he said, "let alone what might come to pass should you be permitted to continue."

"Then it must be between us two," said Det, slowly lowering the scepter and pointing it.

"It always was, was it not?" said Mor.

The Lord of Rondoval hesitated for the barest moment. Then, "I suppose you are right," he said. "But for this, be it upon your own head!"

The scepter flared and a lance of brilliant red light leaped from it. Old Mor leaned forward as it struck full upon the shield his spinning staff had become. The light was instantly reflected upward to strike against the ceiling.

With a roar that outdid the thunder, great chunks of masonry came loose to crash downward upon the Lord of Rondoval, crushing and burying him in an instant.

Mor straightened. The wheel slowed, becoming a staff again. He leaned heavily upon it.

As the echoes died within the hall the remaining sounds of battle came to a halt without. The storm, too, was drifting on its way, its lightnings abated, its thunders stilled in that instant.

One of Jared's lieutenants, Ardel, moved forward slowly and stood regarding the heap of rubble.

"It is over," he said, after a time. "We've won . . ."

"So it would seem," Mor said.

"There are still some of his men about—to be dealt with." Mor nodded.

". . . And the dragons? And his other unnatural servants?"

"Disorganized now," Mor said softly. "I will deal with them."

"Good. We— What is that noise?"

They listened for several moments.

"It could be a trick," said one of the sergeants, Marakas by name.

"Choose a detail. Go and find out. Report back immediately."

Mouseglove crouched behind the arras, near to the stairwell that led to the dark places below. His plan was to return to his cell and secure himself within it. A prisoner of Det's would be about the only person on the premises likely to receive sympathetic treatment, he had reasoned. He had succeeded in making it this far on his journey back to duress when the gate had given way, the invaders entered and the sorcerous duel taken place. He had witnessed all of these things through a frayed place in the tapestry.

Now, while everyone's attention was elsewhere, would be the

ideal time for him to slip out and head back down. Only . . . His curiosity, too, had been aroused. He waited.

The detail soon returned with the noisy bundle. Sergeant Marakas wore a tense expression, held the baby stiffly.

"Doubtless Det planned to sacrifice it in some nefarious rite, to assure his victory," he volunteered.

Ardel leaned forward and inspected. He raised the tiny right hand and turned it palm upwards.

"No. It bears the family's dragon-mark of power inside the right wrist," he stated. "This is Det's own offspring."

"Oh."

Ardel looked at Mor. But the old man was staring at the baby, oblivious to all else.

"What should I do with it, sir?" Marakas asked.

Ardel chewed his lip.

"That mark," he said, "means that it is destined to become a sorcerer. It is also a certain means of identification. No matter what the child might be told while it was growing up, sooner or later it would learn the truth. If that came to pass, would *you* like to meet a sorcerer who knew you had had a part in the death of his father and the destruction of his home?"

"I see what you are getting at . . ." said Marakas.

"So you had best—dispose of—the baby."

The sergeant looked away. Then, "Suppose we sent it to some distant land where no one has ever heard of the House of Rondoval?" he asked.

". . . Where one day there might come a traveler who knows the story? No. The uncertainty would, in many ways, be worse than a sureness of doom. I see no way out for the little thing. Be quick and merciful."

"Sir, could we not just cut off the arm? It is better than dying."

Ardel sighed.

"The power would still be there," he said, "arm or no arm. And there are too many witnesses here today. The story would be told, and it would but add another grievance. No. If you've no stomach for it yourself, there must be someone in the ranks who—"

"Wait!"

Old Mor had spoken. He shook himself as one just awakening and moved forward.

"There may be a way," he said, "a way to let the child live and to assure that your fears will never be realized."

He reached out and touched the tiny hand.

"What do you propose?" Ardel asked him.

"Thousands of years ago," Mor began, "we possessed great cities and mighty machines as well as high magics—"

"I've heard the stories," Ardel said. "How does that help us now?"

"They are more than just stories. The Cataclysm really occurred. Afterwards, we kept the magic and threw much of the rest away. It all seems so much legend now, but to this day we are biased against the unnatural tech-things."

"Of course. That is—"

"Let me finish! When a major decision such as that is made, the symmetry of the universe demands that it go both ways. There is another world, much like our own, where they threw away the magic and kept the other. In that place, we and our ways are the stuff of legend."

"Where is this world?"

Mor smiled.

"It is counterpoint to the music of our sphere," he said, "a single beat away. It is just around the corner no one turns. It is another forking of the shining road."

"Wizards' riddles! How will this serve us? Can one travel to that other place?"

"I can."

"Oh. Then . . ."

"Yes. Growing up in such a place, the child would have its life, but its power would mean little. It would be dismissed, rationalized, explained away. The child would find a different place in life than any it might have known here, and it would never understand, never suspect what had occurred."

"Fine. Do it then, if mercy can be had so cheaply."

"There *is* a price."

"What do you mean?"

"That law of symmetry, of which I spoke—it must be satisfied if the exchange is to be a permanent one: a stone for a stone, a tree for a tree . . ."

"A baby? Are you trying to say that if you take this one there, you must bring one of theirs back?"

"Yes."

"What would we do with that one?"

Sergeant Marakas cleared his throat.

"My Mel and I just lost one," he said. "Perhaps . . ."

Ardel smiled briefly and nodded.

"Then it *is* cheap. Let it be done."

With the toe of his boot and a nod, Ardel then indicated Det's fallen scepter.

"What of the magician's rod? Is it not dangerous?" he asked.

Mor nodded, bent slowly and retrieved it from where it had fallen. He began to twist and tug at it, muttering the while.

"Yes," he finally said, succeeding in separating it into three sections. "It cannot be destroyed, but if I were to banish each segment to a point of the great Magical Triangle of Int, it may be that it will never be reclaimed. It would certainly be difficult."

"You will do this, then?"

"Yes."

At that moment, Mouseglove slipped from behind the arras and down the stairwell. Then he paused, held his breath and listened for an outcry. There was none. He hurried on.

When he reached the dimness of the great stair's bottom, he turned right, took several paces and paused. They were not corridors, but rather natural tunnels that faced him. Had it been the one directly to the right from which he had emerged earlier? Or the other which angled off nearby? He had not realized that there were two in that vicinity . . .

There came a noise from above. He chose the opening on the extreme right and plunged ahead. It was as dark as the route he had traversed earlier, but after twenty paces it took a sharp turn to the right which he did not recall. Still, he could not afford to go back now, if someone were indeed coming. Besides, there was a small light ahead . . .

A brazier of charcoal glowed and smoked within an alcove. A bundle of faggots lay upon the floor nearby. He fed tinder into the brazier, blew upon it, coaxed it to flame. Shortly thereafter, a torch blazed in his hand. He took up several other sticks and continued on along the tunnel.

He came to a branching. The lefthand way looked slightly larger, more inviting. He followed it. Shortly, it branched again. This time, he bore to the right.

He gradually became aware of a downward sloping, thought that he felt a faint draft. There followed three more branchings and a honeycombed chamber. He had begun marking his choices with charcoal from the body of the torch, near to the righthand wall. The incline steepened, the tunnel twisted, widening. It came to bear less and less resemblance to a corridor.

When he halted to light his second torch, he was aware that he had traveled much farther than he had on the way out earlier. Yet he feared returning along the way he had come. A hundred paces more, he decided, could do no harm . . .

And when he had gone that distance, he stood at the mouth of a large, warm cavern, breathing a peculiar odor which he could not identify. He raised the torch high above him, but the farther end of the vast chamber remained hidden in shadows. A hundred paces more, he told himself . . .

Later, when he had decided not to risk further explorations, but to retrace his route and take his chances, he heard an enormous clamor approaching. He realized that he could either throw himself upon the mercy of his fellow men and attempt to explain his situation, or hide himself and extinguish his light. His experience with his fellow men being what it had been, he looked about for an unobtrusive niche.

And that night, the servants of Rondoval were hunted through the wrecked castle and slain. Mor, by his staff and his will, charmed the dragons and other beasts too difficult to slay and drove them into the great caverns beneath. There, he laid the sleep of ages upon everything within and caused the caverns to be sealed.

His next task, he knew, would be at least as difficult.

II.

He walked along the shining road. Miniature lightnings played constantly across its surface but did not shock him. To his right and his left there was a steady flickering as brief glimpses of alternate realities came and went. Directly overhead was a dark stillness filled with steady stars. In his right hand he bore his staff, in the crook of his left arm he carried the baby. Occasionally, there was a branching, a sideroad, a crossroad. He passed many of these with only a glance. Later, however, he came to a forking of the way and he set his foot upon the lefthand branch. Immediately, the flickering slowed perceptibly.

He moved with increased deliberation, now scrutinizing the images. Finally, he concentrated all of his attention on those to the right. After a time, he halted and stood facing the panorama.

He moved his staff into a position before him and the progres-

sion of images slowed even more. He watched for several heart-
beats then leaned the tip of the staff forward.

A scene froze before him, grew, took on depth and colora-
tion . . .

Evening . . . Autumn . . . Small street, small town . . . University complex . . .

He stepped forward.

Michael Chain—red-haired, ruddy and thirty pounds over-
weight—loosened his tie and lowered his six-foot-plus frame onto
the stool before the drawing board. His left hand played games
with the computer terminal and a figure took shape on the
cathode display above it. He studied this for perhaps half a minute, rotated it, made adjustments, rotated it again.

Taking up a pencil and a T-square, he transferred several features from the display to the sheet on the board before him. He
leaned back, regarding it, chewed his lip, began a small erasure.

"Mike!" said a small, dark-haired woman in a severe evening
dress, opening the door to his office. "Can't you leave your work
alone for a minute?"

"The sitter is not here yet," he replied, continuing the erasure,
"and I'm ready to go. This beats twiddling my thumbs."

"Well, she is here now and your tie has to be retied and we're
late."

He sighed, put down the pencil and switched off the terminal.
"All right," he said, rising to his feet and fumbling at his throat.
"I'll be ready in a minute. Punctuality is no great virtue at a fac-
ulty party."

"It is if it's for the head of your department."

"Gloria," he replied, shaking his head, "the only thing you
need to know about Jim is that he wouldn't last a week in the real
world. Take him out of the university and drop him into a genuine industrial design slot and he'd—"

"Let's not get into that again," she said, retreating. "I know
you're not happy here, but for the time being there's nothing else.
You've got to be decent about it."

"My father had his own consulting firm," he recited. "It could have been mine—"

"But he drank it out of business. Come on. Let's go."

"That was near the end. He'd had some bad breaks. He was good. So was Granddad," he went on. "He founded it and—"

"I already know you come from a dynasty of geniuses," she said, "and that Dan will inherit the mantle. But right now—"

He shook himself and looked at her.

"How is he?" he asked in a softer voice.

"Asleep," she said. "He's okay."

He smiled.

"Okay. Let's get our coats. I'll be good."

She turned and he followed her out, the pale eye of the CRT looking over his shoulder.

Mor stood in the doorway of a building diagonally across the street from the house he was watching. The big man in the dark overcoat was on the doorstep, hands thrust into his pockets, gazing up the street. The smaller figure of the woman still faced the partly opened door. She was speaking with someone within.

Finally, the woman closed the door and turned. She joined the man and they began walking. Mor watched them head off up the street and turn the corner. He waited awhile longer, to be certain they would not be returning after some remembered trifle.

He departed the doorway and crossed the street. When he reached the proper door he rapped upon it with his staff.

After several moments, the door opened slightly. He saw that there was a chain upon it on the inside. A young girl stared at him across it, dark eyes only slightly suspicious.

"I've come to pick something up," he said, the web of an earlier spell making his foreign words clear to her, "and to leave something."

"They are not in just now," she said. "I'm the sitter . . ."

"That is all right," he said, slowly lowering the point of his staff toward her eye level.

A faint pulsing began within the dark wood, giving it an opalescent hue and texture. Her eyes shifted. It held her attention for several pulsebeats, and then he raised it slowly toward his own face. Their eyes met and he held her gaze. His voice shifted into a lower register.

"Unchain the door now," he said.

There was a shadow of movement, a rattling within. The chain dropped.

"Step back," he commanded.

The face withdrew. He pushed the door open and entered.

"Go into the next room and sit down," he said, closing the door behind him. "When I depart this place, you will chain the door behind me and forget that I had been here. I will tell you when to do this."

The girl was already on her way into the living room.

He moved about slowly, opening doors. Finally, he paused upon the threshold of a small, darkened room, then entered softly. He regarded the tiny figure curled within the crib, then moved the staff to within inches of its head.

"Sleep," he said, the wood once again flickering beneath his hand. "Sleep."

Carefully then, he placed his own burden upon the floor, leaned his staff against the crib, uncovered and raised the child he had charmed. He lay it beside the other and considered them both. In the light that spilled through the opened door, he saw that this baby was lighter of complexion than the one he had brought, and its hair was somewhat thinner, paler. Still . . .

He proceeded to exchange their clothing and to wrap the baby from the crib in the blanket which had covered the other. Then he placed the last Lord of Rondoval within the crib and stared at him. His finger moved forward to touch the dragonmark . . .

Abruptly, he turned away, retrieved his staff and lifted young Daniel Chain from the floor.

As he passed along the hallway he called into the living room, "I am going now. Fix the door as it was after me—and forget."

Outside, he heard the chain fall into place as he walked away. Stars shone down through jagged openings among the clouds and a cold wind came out of the east at his back. A vehicle turned the corner, raking him with its lights, but it passed without slowing.

Tiny gleams began to play within the sidewalk, and the buildings at either hand lost something of their substantiality, became two-dimensional, began to flicker.

The sparkling of his path increased and it soon ceased to be a sidewalk, becoming a great bright way stretching illimitably before and behind him, with numerous sideways visible. The prospect to his right and left became a mosaic of tiny still-shots of innumerable times and places, flashing, brightening and shrinking, coming at last to resemble the shimmering scales of some exotic fish in passage by him. Overhead, a band of dark sky remained, but cloudless and pouring starlight in negative celestial image of the road below. Occasionally, Mor glimpsed other figures upon the sideways—not all of them of human form—bent on tasks as inscrutable as his own.

His staff came to blaze as he picked his way homeward, lightning-dew dripping from his heels, his toes.

III.

In lands mythical to one another, the days passed.

When the boy was six years old, it was noted that he not only attempted to repair anything that was broken about the place, but that he quite often succeeded. Mel showed her husband the kitchen tongs he had mended.

"As good as Vince could have done at the smithy," she said. "That boy's going to be a tinker."

Marakas examined the tool.

"Did you see how he did it?" he asked.

"No. I heard his hammering, but I didn't pay him much heed. You know how he's always fooling with bits of metal and such."

Marakas nodded and set the tongs aside.

"Where is he now?"

"Down by the irrigation ditch, I think," she answered. "He splashes about there."

"I'll walk down and see him, tell him he was a good boy for mending that," he said, crossing the room and lifting the latch.

Outside, he turned the corner and took the sloping path past the huge tree in the direction of the fields. Insects buzzed in the grasses. A bird warbled somewhere above him. A dry breeze stirred his hair. As he walked, he thought somewhat proudly of the child they had taken. He was certainly healthy and strong— and very clever . . .

"Mark?" he called when he had reached the ditch.

"Over here, Dad," came a faint reply from around the bend to his right.

He moved in that direction.

"Where?" he asked, after a time.

"Down here."

Approaching the edge, he looked over, seeing Mark and the thing with which he was playing. It appeared that the boy had placed a smooth, straight stick just above the water's surface, resting each of its ends loosely in grooves among rock heaps he had built up on either side; and at the middle of the stick was affixed a series of squarish—wings?—which the flowing water pushed against, turning it round and round. A peculiar tingle of trepidation passed over him at the sight of it—why, he was not certain—but this vanished moments later as he followed the rotating vanes with his eyes, becoming a sense of pleasure at his son's achievement.

"What have you got there, Mark?" he asked, seating himself on the bank.

"Just a sort of—wheel," the boy said, looking up and smiling. "The water turns it."

"What does it do?"

"Nothing. Just turns."

"It's real pretty."

"Yeah, isn't it?"

"That was nice the way you fixed those tongs," Marakas said, plucking a piece of grass and chewing it. "Your mother liked that."

"It was easy."

"You enjoy fixing things and making things, making things work—don't you?"

"Yes."

"Think that's what you'd like to do for a living some day?"

"I think so."

"Old Vince is going to be looking for an apprentice down at the forge one of these days. If you think you'd like to learn smithing, working with metals and such—I could speak with him."

Mark smiled again.

"Do that," he said.

"Of course, you'd be working with real, practical things." Marakas gestured toward the water-spun wheel. "Not toys," he finished.

"It isn't a toy," Mark said, turning to look back at his creation.

"You just said that it doesn't do anything."

"But I think it could. I just have to figure what—and how."

Marakas laughed, stood and stretched. He tossed his blade of grass into the water and watched the wheel mangle it.

"When you find out, be sure to tell me."

He turned away and started back toward the path.

"I will . . ." Mark said softly, still watching it turn.

When the boy was six years old, he went into his father's office to see once again the funny machine Dad used. Maybe this time—

"Dan! Get out of here!" bellowed Michael Chain, a huge figure, without even turning away from the drawing board.

The little stick figure on the screen before him had collapsed into a line that waved up and down. Michael's hand played across the console, attempting adjustments.

"Gloria! Come and get him! It's happening again!"

"Dad," Dan began, "I didn't mean—"

The man swiveled and glared at him.

"I've told you to stay out of here when I'm working," he said.

"I know. But I thought that maybe this time—"

"You thought! You thought! It's time you started doing what you're told!"

"I'm sor—"

Michael Chain began to rise from his stool and the boy backed away. Then Dan heard his mother's footsteps at his back. He turned and hugged her.

"I'm sorry," he finished.

"Again?" Gloria said, looking over him at her husband.

"Again," Michael answered. "The kid's a jinx."

The pencil-can began rattling atop the small table beside the drawing board. Michael turned and stared at it, fascinated. It tipped, fell to its side, rolled toward the table's edge.

He lunged, but it passed over the edge and fell to the floor before he could reach it. Cursing, he straightened then and banged his head on the nearest corner.

"Get him out of here!" he roared. "The kid's got a pet poltergeist!"

"Come on," Gloria said, leading him away. "We know it's not something you want to do . . ."

The window blew open. Papers swirled. There came a sharp rapping from within the wall. A book fell from its shelf.

". . . It's just something that sometimes happens," she finished, as they departed.

Michael sighed, picked things up, rose, closed the window. When he returned to his machine, it was functioning normally. He glared at it. He did not like things that he could not understand. Was it a wave phenomenon that the kid propagated—intensified somehow when he became upset? He had tried several times to detect something of that sort, using various instruments. Always unsuccessfully. The instruments themselves usually—

"Now you've done it. He's crying and the place is a shambles," Gloria said, entering the room again. "If you'd be a little more gentle with him when it starts, things probably wouldn't get so bad. *I* can usually head them off, just by being nice to him."

"In the first place," Michael said, "I'm not sure I believe that anything paranormal really happens. In the second, it's always so sudden."

She laughed. So did he.

"Well, it is," he said finally. "I suppose I had better go and say something to him. I know it's not his fault. I don't want him unhappy . . ."

He had started toward the door. He paused.

"I still wonder," he said.

"I know."

"I'm sure our kid didn't have that funny mark on his wrist."

"Don't start that again. Please. It just takes you around in circles."

"You're right."

He departed his office and walked back toward Dan's room. As he went, he heard the sounds of a guitar being softly strummed. Now a D chord, now a G . . . Surprising, how quickly a kid that age had learned to handle the undersized instrument . . . Strange, too. No one else in either family had ever shown any musical aptitude.

He knocked gently on the door. The strumming stopped.

"Yes?"

"May I come in?"

"Uh-huh."

He pushed the door open and entered. Dan was sprawled on the bed. The instrument was nowhere in sight. Underneath, probably.

"That was real pretty," he said. "What were you playing?"

"Just some sounds. I don't know."

"Why'd you stop?"

"You don't like it."

"I never said that."

"I can tell."

He sat down beside him and squeezed his shoulder.

"Well, you're wrong," he said. "Everybody's got something they like to do. With me, it's my work." Then, finally, "You scared me, Dan. I don't know how it happens that machines sometimes go crazy when you come around—and things I don't understand sometimes scare me. But I'm not really mad at you. I just sound that way when I'm startled."

Dan rolled onto his side and looked up at him. He smiled weakly.

"You want to play something for me? I'll be glad to listen."

The boy shook his head.

"Not just now," he said.

Michael looked about the room, at the huge shelf of picture books, at the unopened erector set. When he looked back at Dan, he saw that the boy was rubbing his wrist.

"Hurt your hand?" he asked.

"Uh-uh. It just sort of throbs—the mark—sometimes."

"How often?"

"Whenever—something like that—happens."

He gestured toward the door and the entire external world.

"It's going away now," he added.

He took hold of the boy's wrist, examined the dark dragon-shape upon it.

"The doctor said it was nothing to worry about—no chance of it ever turning into anything bad . . ."

"It's all right now."

Michael continued to stare for several moments. Finally, he squeezed the hand, lowered it and smiled.

"Anything you want, Dan?" he asked.

"No. Uh . . . Well—some books.

Michael laughed.

"That's one thing you like, isn't it? Okay, maybe we can stop by a bookstore later and see what they've got."

Dan finally smiled.

"Thank you."

Michael punched his shoulder lightly and rose.

". . . And I'll stay out of your office, Dad."

He squeezed his shoulder again and left him there on the bed. As he headed back toward his office, he heard a soft, rapid strumming begin.

When the boy was twelve years old he built a horse. It stood two hands high and was moved by a spring-powered clockwork mechanism. He had worked after hours at the smithy forging the parts, and on his own time in the shed he had built behind his parents' place, measuring, grinding and polishing gears. Now it pranced on the floor of that shed, for him and his audience of one —Nora Vail, a nine-year-old neighbor girl.

She clapped her hands as it slowly turned its head, as if to regard them.

"It's beautiful, Mark! It's beautiful!" she said. "There's never been anything like it—except in the old days."

"What do you mean?" he said quickly.

"You know. Like long ago. When they had all sorts of clever devices like that."

"Those are just stories," he said. Then, after a time, "Aren't they?"

She shook her head, pale hair dancing.

"No. My father's passed by one of the forbidden places, down south by Anvil Mountain. You can still see all sorts of broken things there without going in—things people can't make anymore." She looked back at the horse, its movements now slowing. "Maybe even things like that."

"That's—interesting . . ." he said. "I didn't realize— And there's still stuff left?"

"That's what my father said."

Abruptly, she looked him straight in the eye.

"You know, maybe you'd better not show this to anybody else," she said.

"Why not?"

"People might think you've been there and learned some of the forbidden things. They might get mad."

"That's dumb," he said, just as the horse fell onto its side. "That's real dumb."

But as he righted it, he said, "Maybe I'll wait till I have something better to show them. Something they'll like . . ."

The following spring, he demonstrated for a few friends and
neighbors the flotation device he had made, geared to operate a
floodgate in the irrigation system. They talked about it for two
weeks, then decided against installing it themselves. When the
spring runoff occurred—and later, when the rains came—there
was some local flooding, not too serious. They only shrugged.

"I'll have to show them something even better," he told Nora.
"Something they'll *have* to like."

"Why?" she asked.

He looked at her, puzzled.

"Because they have to understand," he said.

"What?"

"That I'm right and they're wrong, of course."

"People don't usually go for that sort of thing," she said.

He smiled.

"We'll see."

When the boy was twelve years old, he took his guitar with him
one day—as he had on many others—and visited a small park
deep in the steel, glass, plastic and concrete-lined heart of the city
where his family now resided.

He patted a dusty synthetic tree and crossed the unliving turf
past holograms of swaying flowers, to seat himself upon an orange plastic bench. Recordings of birdsongs sounded at random
intervals through hidden speakers. Artificial butterflies darted
along invisible beams. Concealed aerosols released the odors of
flowers at regular intervals.

He removed the instrument from its case and tuned it. He
began to play.

One of the fake butterflies passed too near, faltered and fell to
the ground. He stopped playing and leaned forward to examine it.
A woman passed and tossed a coin near his feet. He straightened
and ran a hand through his hair, staring after her. The disarrayed
silver-white streak that traced his black mop from forehead to
nape fell into place again.

He rested the guitar on his thigh, chorded and began an intricate right-hand style he had been practicing. A dark form—a real bird—suddenly descended, to hop about nearby. Dan almost stopped playing at the novel sight. Instead, he switched to a simpler style, to leave more attention for its movements.

Sometimes at night he played his guitar on the roof of the building where birds nested, beneath stars twinkling faintly through the haze. He would hear them twittering and rustling about him. But he seldom saw any in the parks—perhaps it was something in the aerosols—and he watched this one with a small fascination as it approached the failed butterfly and seized it in its beak. A moment later, it dropped it, cocked its head, pecked at it, then hopped away. Shortly thereafter, the bird was airborne once again, then gone.

Dan reverted to a more complex pattern, and after a time he began singing against the noises of the city. The sun passed redly overhead. A wino, sprawled beneath the level of the holograms, sobbed softly in his sleep. The park vibrated regularly with the passage of underground trains. After several lapses, Dan realized that his voice was changing.

IV.

Mark Marakson—six feet in height and still growing, muscles as hard as any smith's—wiped his hands on his apron, brushed his unruly thatch of red back from his forehead and mounted the device.

He checked the firebox again, made a final adjustment on the boiler and seated himself before the steering mechanism. The vehicle whistled and banged as he released the clutch and drove it out of his hidden shed, heading down toward the roadway along the path he had smoothed.

Birds, rabbits and squirrels fled before him, and he smiled at the power beneath his hands. He took a corner sharply, enjoying the response to the controls. This was the sixth trial of his self-propelled wagon and everything seemed to be functioning perfectly. The first five expeditions had been secret things. But now . . .

He laughed aloud. Yes, now was the time to surprise the villagers, to show them what could be wrought with thinking and ingenuity. He checked the pressure gauge at his side. Fine . . .

And it was a beautiful morning for such an expedition—sunny, breezy, the spring flowers in bloom at either hand . . . His heart leaped within him as the hardwood seat pounded his backside and thoughts of suspension systems danced through his mind. It was indeed a day for great undertakings.

He chugged along, occasionally feeding the flames, trying to imagine the expressions on the people's faces when they got their first sight of the contraption. A farmer in a distant field let up his plowing and stared, but he was too far removed for his reaction to be visible. Mark wished suddenly that he had thought to install some sort of whistle or bell.

As he neared the village, he drew back on the brake, slowing. He planned to halt right in the middle of town, stand on the seat and give a little talk. "Get rid of your horses," it would begin. "A new day is dawning . . ."

He heard the cries of children from a nearby field. Soon they were racing along beside him, screaming questions. He tried to answer them, but the noises of the machine destroyed his words.

As he turned onto the only street through the village, slowing even more, a horse bolted and ran off between two houses, dragging a small cart. He saw people running and heard doors slamming. Dogs snarled, barked and backed away. The children kept pace.

Reaching the town's center, he braked to a complete halt and looked about.

"Can we ride on it?" the children shouted.

"Maybe later," he replied, turning to check that everything was still in good order.

Doors began to open. People emerged from homes and stables to stand staring at him. Their expressions were not at all what he had imagined they would be. Some were blank-faced, many seemed fearful, a few looked angry.

"What is it?" a man shouted from across the way.

"A steam wagon," he yelled back. "It—"

"Get it out of here!" someone else called. "We'll all be cursed!"

"It's not bad magic—" he began.

"Get it out!"

"Out with it!"

"Bringing that damned thing into town . . ."

A clod of earth struck the side of the boiler.

"You don't understand!"

"Out! Out! Out!"

Stones began to fly. A number of men began moving toward him. He singled out the one he knew best.

"Jed!" he shouted. "It's not bad magic! It's just like boiling water to make tea!"

Jed did not reply, but reached out with the others to seize hold of the wagon's quivering side.

"We'll boil you, you bastard!" one of the others shouted, and they began to rock the vehicle.

"Stop! Stop! You'll damage it!" Mark cried.

Topheavy, it quickly responded to their pressures with a swaying motion. When he realized that it was beginning to tip, it was too late to jump.

"Damn you!" he cried, and he fell.

He landed rolling and struck his head but did not pass out. Dazed, he saw the boiler burst and the firebox come open, scattering embers. Several droplets of hot spray struck him, and he continued to roll. The waters streamed off toward the main ditch, missing him.

"Damn you, damn you, damn you, damn you," he heard himself repeating, and then he blacked out.

He smelled the smoke and heard the flames when he came around again. The wagon had taken fire from the embers. People stood about watching it burn. No one made an attempt to extinguish it.

". . . Have to get a wise man to exorcise the demon now," he overheard a woman saying. "Don't no one touch it. You kids stay away!"

"Fools!" he muttered, and he struggled to rise.

A small hand on his shoulder pushed him back.

"No! Don't draw attention to yourself! Just lie still!"

"Nora . . . ?"

He looked up. He had not at first realized that she was there, holding a compress to his head.

"Yes. Rest a moment. Gather your strength. Then come back this way between the houses." She gestured with her head. "We'll move quickly when we do."

"They didn't understand . . ."

"I know. I know. It was like the horse, when we were children . . ."

"Yes."

". . . Something you just thought up because you think that way. I understand."

"Damn them!" he said.

"No. They just don't think the way you do."

"I'll show them!"

"Not now you won't. Let's just get ready and slip away. After that, I think it might be a good idea for you to stay out of sight for a time."

He stared at the burning wagon and at the faces beyond it.

"I suppose you are right," he said. "Damn them. I'm ready. I want to get out of here."

She took hold of his hand. He winced and drew it back.

"I'm sorry. It's burned," she said. "I hadn't noticed."

"Neither had I. It will be all right, though. Let's go."

She clasped his other hand. He rose quickly and moved with her, past shrubs, beyond the houses.

"This way."

He followed her down a lane, through a barn.

When they paused to rest, he said, "Thank you. You were right. I'm going away for awhile."

"Where?"

"South," he hissed.

"Oh, no!" she said. "That's too wild, and—"

"I've got the name," he stated.

She stared into his eyes.

"Don't," she said.

He reached forward and embraced her. She was stiff for a moment, then relaxed against him.

"I'll be back for you," he told her.

The trees were smaller, the land was drier here. There were fewer shrubs and more bare areas. This land was rockier and much, much quieter than his own. He heard no birdcalls as he walked and climbed, no insect-noises, no sounds of running water, rustling boughs, passing animals.

His hand had stopped throbbing several days ago, and the skin was peeling now. He had long since discarded the bandage from his head. His tread was firm despite weariness, as he neared the anvil-shaped peak through lengthening shadows. He wore a small backpack, and several well-wrapped water bottles hung from his belt. His garments were dirty, as were his face and hands, but he smiled a tight smile as he looked upward and plodded on.

He did not feel that there were demons and assorted monsters in the area, as some people believed. But he bore a short sword across his pack—one he had forged himself years before, when he had been shorter and lighter. It seemed almost a toy now, though he could wield it with great speed and dexterity. He had spent months practicing with blades to obtain the feeling for edged weapons which alone would insure his producing a superior product when he came to forge them. He had picked his up at the smithy when he had returned there for the supplies for his flight. Now, hiking closer and closer to the forbidden area, he felt no great need for the blade in what he took to be a dead place, but its presence made him think of the effort which had gone into its manufacture yet had still produced an item inferior in quality to some of the strange fragments of metal he discovered imbedded in the ground here.

He carried such a scrap in his hand and studied it now and again. He saw it to be some sort of tough, light alloy, once he had scraped and rubbed the dirt from it, uncorrupted after all these years. What were the forces that had formed it? What heats? What pressures? It told him that something peculiar had once existed nearby.

That evening he walked through the still standing shell of a large building. He could not even guess what might once have been transacted within it. But twice he thought that he heard scurrying sounds near at hand as he explored. He decided to camp at some distance from the ruin.

He could not decide whether a fire would attract or repel anything that might dwell nearby. Finally, the lack of sufficient kindling materials to keep a blaze going for very long persuaded him to do entirely without. He ate dry rations and rolled himself into his blanket on a ledge eight feet above the ground. He placed his blade within easy reach.

How long he had slept, he could not say. Several hours, it felt, when he was awakened by a scratching noise. He was alert in an instant, hand moving toward the weapon. He turned his head slightly, muscles tensing, and beheld the thing which moved over the rocks below, coming in his direction.

Its dark, segmented body gleamed in the moonlight as it crept

over the rocks on numerous tiny feet, its front end sometimes raised, sometimes lowered. It was three or four times his own size, and it resembled nothing so much as a gigantic, metallic caterpillar moving along the trail he had followed to this place. Mounted near the forward end was something small and twisted and vaguely man-shaped, clutching what appeared to be reins in its left hand and the shaft of a long spear in the other. The beast reared, rising as high as the ledge, swayed, then dropped to the ground once more and proceeded as if sniffing out his path.

Hackles risen, a cold lump in the pit of his stomach, Mark eyed a possible escape route among the rocks below and to the right. If he moved quickly enough there might still be a sufficient margin . . .

He breathed deeply, vaulted to the ground and twisted his ankle beneath him. Rising, limping, he headed toward the rocks. He heard a sharp whistling noise behind him and an increase in the scratching sounds. He dodged as best he could, thinking of the spear in the thing's hand.

He looked back once and saw that he seemed to be holding his own. The spear-arm was cocked, but the rocks were right before him now. He dove and heard the shaft clatter on stone behind him. Recovering immediately, he continued on, heading obliquely back in the direction of the ruin he had visited earlier.

The noises behind him did not diminish. Apparently, the monstrosity could move at a faster pace than that at which he had first seen it coming.

He darted among rocks, keeping the sounds to the rear and the ruin roughly ahead. There had been places to climb, places to hide there—places better suited for defense than the open ground of this rock maze.

He rounded a huge boulder, froze, and barely had time to bring his blade into play. Another of the things, also bearing a rider, appeared to have been searching or waiting for him. It was reared upright only feet away, and the spear was already descending.

He parried, driving the shaft aside, and swung a backhanded cut toward the swaying creature. It rang like a bell and dropped forward. He stepped aside, feeling a sharp pain in his right ankle,

then thrust upward toward the gnarled rider. There came a
scream as his blade connected and entered, somewhere. He
dragged it free, turned, ran.

There were no sounds of pursuit, and when he glanced back he
saw the beast, now riderless, groping aimlessly among the rocks.
He began to draw a deep breath, and then the world gave way beneath him. He fell a short distance through darkness and landed
shoulder-first on a hard surface. The blade fell from his hand with
a clanging sound, and he immediately retrieved it. There came a
sharp, slamming noise from overhead, and dust, gravel and pieces
of earth fell about him. Suddenly then, there was light, but his
eyes did not immediately adjust to it.

When the effects of the brightness had passed, he still did not
understand what lay before him.

A table . . . Yes, he recognized that—and the chairs. But
where was the main light source? What was that large gray thing
with the glassy rectangle at its center? And all those tiny lights?

Nothing moved about him, save for the settling dust. He got to
his feet, advancing slowly.

"Hello?" he whispered.

"Yes, hello, hello!" came a loud voice. "Hello?"

"Where are you?" he asked, halting and turning in a slow circle.

"Here, with you," was the reply. The words had an archaic ac-
cent to them, like that of the Northlanders.

"I do not see you. Who are you?"

"My, you speak strangely! Foreigner? I am a teaching machine,
a library computer."

"My words may seem strangely accented and assembled because of the passage of time," Mark said, with a sudden insight
concerning the age and function of the device. "Can you make al-
lowances, adjust for this? I am having a difficult time understanding even your simplest statements."

"Yes. Talk a lot. I need a good sample. Tell me about yourself
and the things that you wish to know."

Mark smiled and lowered his blade. He limped to the nearest
chair and slumped into it. He rubbed his shoulder.

"I will," he said, moments later. "But how is this place lighted?"

The screen glowed before him. Beneath a heavy layer of dust, a wiring diagram suddenly appeared upon it.

"Is that what you mean?" asked the voice.

"Maybe. I'm not certain."

"Do you know what it is?"

"Not yet," he said, "but I intend to. If you will instruct me."

"I have the means to provide for your well-being for so long as you wish to remain here. I will instruct you."

"I think I may have just fallen into the very thing I sought," Mark replied. "I'll tell you about myself, and you tell me about power sources . . ."

V.

Daniel Chain—a Junior at State, working on his certificate in Medieval Studies; slim and hard, after two years on the boxing and fencing teams; less than happy, at the subtle pressure still exerted by his father for him to change his History and Linguistics major and join him in the business—sat upon the tall stool, thinking of all these matters and others, after the fashion of half-controlled reverie which informed his mind whenever he played.

The club was dim and smoky. He had followed Betty Lewis, who sang torch songs and blues numbers accompanied by piano rolls and a deep decolletage and who always drew heavy applause when she took her bows. Now he was filling the room with guitar sounds. He played on Saturday nights and alternate Fridays, doing as many instrumentals as vocals. The people seemed to like his music both ways. Right now, he was in a nonvocal mood.

Tonight was the other Friday, and the place was considerably less than packed. He recognized several familiar faces at the small tables, some of them nodding in time with the beat.

He sculpted the swirls of smoke as they drifted up toward the lights, into castles, mountain ranges, forests and exotic beasts. The mark on his wrist throbbed slightly as this occurred. It was strange how few of the patrons ever looked up and noticed his music-shaped daydreams hovering above their heads. Or perhaps the ones who did were already high and thought it normal.

Improvising, he moved an army across a ridge. He attacked it with dragons and tore it to pieces. Troops fled in all directions. Smiling, he upped the tempo.

In time, he saw an elbow strike a mug of beer. It slowed in midair as he played, twisting upright, retaining much of the beverage. It came to a stop inches above the floor, then descended the final distance gently. By the time its owner found it there and exclaimed upon the miracle, Dan had returned to his world of open spaces and trees, mountains and clear rivers, prancing unicorns and diving griffins.

Jerry, the bartender, sent up a pint. Dan paused to sip from it,

then in a small fit of self-awareness began the tune to which he had set "Miniver Cheevy." Soon, he was singing the words.

Somewhere past the halfway point, he noticed a frightened look on Jerry's face. He had just taken a step backward. The man immediately before him was leaning forward, hunched over his drink and looking ahead. By leaning back on the stool and craning his neck, Dan could just make out the lines of the small handgun the man held, partly wrapped in a handkerchief. He had never tried to stop one from firing and wondered whether he could. Of course, the trigger might well remain untugged. Jerry was already turning slowly toward the cash register.

The pulse in his right wrist deepened as he stared at a heavy mug and watched it slide along the bartop, as he shifted his gaze to an empty chair and saw it begin to creep forward. For those moments, a part of him seemed also to be a part of the chair and the mug.

Jerry rang up NO SALE and was counting out the bills from the register. The chair found its position behind the hunched gunman and halted, soundlessly. Dan sang on, castles fallen, dragons flown, troops scattered in the white haze about the lights.

Jerry returned to the counter and passed the man a wad of bills. They vanished quickly into a jacket pocket. The weapon was now completely covered by the handkerchief. The man straightened and slid from the stool, eyes and weapon still upon the bartender. As he moved backward and began to turn the chair lurched to reposition itself. His foot struck it and he stumbled, throwing out his hands to save himself.

As he sprawled, the mug rose from the counter and sped toward his head. When it connected, he lay still. The weapon in its white wrapping sped across the floor to vanish beneath the performer's platform in the corner.

Dan finished his song and took another drink. Jerry was beside the man, recovering the money. A knot of people had already formed at that end of the room.

"That was very strange."

He turned his head. It was Betty Lewis who had spoken. She

had left the table near the wall where she had been sitting, sipping something, and approached the platform.

"What was strange?" he said.

"I saw that chair move by itself—the one he tripped on."

"Probably someone bumped it."

"No."

Now she was looking at him rather than the scene across the room.

"The whole thing was very peculiar. The mug . . ." she said. "Funny things seem to happen when you're playing. Usually little things. Sometimes it's just a feeling."

He smiled.

"It's called mood. I'm a great artist."

He fingered a chord, ran an arpeggio. She laughed.

"No, I think you're haunted."

He nodded.

"Like Cheevy. By visions."

"Nobody's listening now," she said. "Let's sit down."

"Okay."

He leaned his guitar against the stool and took his beer to her table.

"You write a lot of your own stuff, don't you?" she said, after they had seated themselves.

"Yes."

"I like your music and your voice. Maybe we could work out a thing where we do a couple of numbers together."

"Maybe," he said, "if you've no objection to the strange things you say happen."

"I like strange things." She reached out and touched his hair. "That's real, isn't it—the streak?"

"Yes."

"At first I thought—you were a little weird."

". . . And now you know it?"

She laughed.

"I suppose so. Someone said you're still in school? That right?"

"It is."

"You going to stay with music when you get out?"

He shrugged.

"Hard to say."

"You've got a future, I'd think. Ever record anything?"

"No."

"I had a record. Didn't do well."

"Sorry."

"The breaks . . . Maybe bad timing. Maybe not, too. I don't know. I'd really like to try something with you. See how it sounds. If it works, I know a guy . . ."

"My material?"

"Yeah."

He nodded.

"Okay. After the show, let's go somewhere and try a few."

"My place isn't far. We can walk."

"Fine."

He took a sip of beer, glanced over and saw that the man on the floor was beginning to stir. In the distance, he heard the sound of a siren. He heard someone ask, "Where's the gun?"

"It's a funny feeling I get when I hear you," she resumed, "as though the world were a little bit out of kilter."

"Maybe it is."

". . . As though you tear a little hole through it and I can see a piece of something else on the other side."

"If I could only tear one big enough I'd step through."

"You sound like my ex-husband."

"Was he a musician?"

"No. He was a physicist who liked poetry."

"What became of him?"

"He's out on the Coast in a commune. Arts and crafts, gardening . . . Stuff like that."

"He up and leave, or he ask you to go with?"

"He asked, but I didn't want pig shit on my heels."

Dan nodded.

"I'll have to watch where I step if I ever step through."

The police car pulled up in front, its light turning, blinking. The siren died. Dan finished his drink as someone located the weapon.

"We'd look pretty good on an album cover," she said. "Especially with that streak. Maybe I could . . . Naw."

The man with the sore head was led away. Car doors slammed. The blinking stopped.

"I've got to go sing something," he said, rising. "Or is it your turn?"

She looked at her watch.

"You finish up," she said. "I'll just listen and wait."

He mounted the platform and took the guitar into his hands. The pillars of smoke began to intertwine.

VI.

The giant mechanical bird deposited Mark Marakson on the hilltop. Mark brushed back the soft green sleeve of his upper garment and pressed several buttons on the wide bracelet he wore upon his left wrist. The bird took flight again, climbing steadily. He controlled its passage with the wristband and saw through its eyes upon the tiny screen at the bracelet's center.

He saw that the way ahead was clear. He shouldered his pack and began walking. Down from the hill and through the woods he went, coming at last to a trail that led toward more open country. Overhead, his bird was but a tiny dot, circling high above.

He passed cultivated fields, but no habitations until he came within sight of his father's house. He had plotted his return route carefully.

His workshed stood undisturbed. He deposited his pack within it and headed toward the house.

The door swung shut behind him. The place seemed more disarrayed than he had ever before seen it.

"Hello!" he called. "Hello?"

There was no reply. He went through the entire house, finding no one. Dust lay thick everywhere. Marakas could well be in the field, or tending to any of the numerous chores about the place. But Melanie was usually in the house. He looked about outside, investigating the barns and worksheds, walked down to the ditches, scanned the fields. No one. He returned to the house and sought food for lunch. The larder was empty, however, so he ate of his own provisions. But he operated the wrist-control first, and the speck in the heavens ceased its circling and sped southward.

Disturbed, he began cleaning and straightening about the place. Finally, he went out to the shed and set to work assembling the unit he had brought with him.

It was on toward evening, his labors long finished, when he heard the sound of the approaching wagon. He departed the house, which he had set back in order, and awaited the vehicle's arrival.

He saw Marakas drive up to the barn and begin unhitching the team. He walked over to assist him.

"Dad . . ." he said. "Hello."

Marakas turned and stared at him. His expression remained blank for an instant too long. During that instant, it struck Mark what had troubled him about his father's movements, his reaction time: he was more than a little drunk.

"Mark," he said then, recognition spreading across his face. He took a small step forward. "You've been gone. Over a year. A year and a half . . . Almost two. What—happened? Where have you been?"

"It's a long story. Here, let me help with that."

He took over the unhitching of the team, the rubbing down of the horses in their stalls, their feeding.

". . . So, when they destroyed my wagon, I had to leave. I was —afraid. I headed south."

He barred the barn door. The sun was just losing its final edge.

"But so long, Mark . . . You never sent us word or anything," Marakas said.

"I couldn't. How's—how's mother?"

Marakas looked away and did not reply. Finally, he pointed toward a small orchard.

"Over there," he said at last.

After a time, Mark asked, "How'd it happen?"

"In her sleep. It wasn't bad for her. Come on."

They walked toward the orchard. Mark saw the small, rocked-over grave, a part of the shadows and rootwork near one of the larger trees. He halted beside it, looking down.

"My going away . . ." he finally said. "That didn't have anything to do with it—did it?"

Marakas put a hand on his shoulder.

"No, of course not."

"You never appreciate . . . Till they're gone."

"I know."

"That's why the place is—not the way it used to be?"

"It's no secret I've been drinking a lot. Yes. My heart hasn't been in things around here."

Mark nodded, dropped to one knee, touched the stones.

"We could work the place together, now you're back," Marakas said.

"I can't."

"They've got another smith now. New fellow."

"I didn't want to do that either."

"What will you be doing?"

"Something new, different. That's a long story, too. Mother—"

His voice broke, and he was silent for a long while.

Finally, "Mark, I don't think too clearly when I've been drinking," Marakas said, "and I don't know whether I ought to tell you this now, later or never. You loved her and she loved you, and I don't know . . ."

"What?"

"I guess a man should know, sometime, and you're a man now, and things'd of been a lot different without you. We wanted a kid, see?"

Mark rose slowly.

"What do you mean?"

"I'm not your father. She's not your mother. Natural-like, I mean."

"I don't understand . . ."

"We never had any of our own that lived. It was a sad thing. So when we had a chance to make a home for a baby, we took it."

"Then, who were my natural parents?"

"I don't know. It was right after the war—"

"I was orphaned?"

"I don't think so. I couldn't understand all the wizard's fancy talk. But they couldn't bring themselves to kill old Devil Det's kid, so they sent him someplace far away and got you in exchange. He called you a changeling. That's all I know. We were so glad to take you. Mel's life was a lot happier than it would have been otherwise. Mine, too. I hope that doesn't change anything between us. But I felt it was time for you to know."

Mark embraced him.

"You wanted me," he said, a little later. "That's more than a lot of people can say."

"It's good to see you again. Let's go back to the house. There's some food and stuff in the wagon."

After dinner, they finished a bottle of wine and Marakas grew sleepy. Shortly after he had retired, Mark returned to his shed. They should all be circling high above now, he realized, bearing the additional equipment he needed, awaiting the signal to bring it to him. He carried the unit he had assembled earlier to a large, open area, from which he transmitted the necessary orders.

The dark bird-shapes began drifting down out of the sky, blotting out stars, their outlines growing to vast proportions. He smiled.

It took him several hours to unload the equipment and convey most of it to the barn. He was bone-tired when he had finished. He sent all but one of these products of his assembly lines flying back to his city in the south. That one he set to circling again, at a great altitude.

He returned to his shed to sleep, pausing in the orchard a final time.

The following day, Mark assembled a small vehicle which, he explained to Marakas, drew its energy from the sun. He could not convince him that this was not a form of magic. That he did not wish to explain from where the parts had come only added to this impression. Mark gave up when he saw that it did not seem to matter to Marakas, and he went on with the installation of special features. That afternoon, he loaded it with equipment and drove off along the trail that followed the canal. He returned several times for additional tools and equipment.

For the next five days, he remained away from the farm. The afternoon that his work was completed, he drove toward the village. He headed the car down its street and halted it at the same spot where his steam wagon had been destroyed. He activated several circuits and picked up the microphone.

"This is Mark Marakson," he said, and his voice rang through

the town. "I've returned to tell you some of the things to which
you would not listen before—and many new things, as well . . ."

Faces appeared at windows. Doors began to open.

"This wagon, like the other, is not powered by a demon. It uses
natural energies to do work. I can build planting and plowing and
harvesting devices of similar design which will function faster and
more efficiently than any a horse can draw. In fact, I already
have. I propose to furnish these for no charge to all of the farms
in the area and to provide instruction in their use. I would like to
turn our land into a model of scientific farming techniques, and
then into a manufacturing center for these vehicles. We will all
grow rich, providing them to the rest of the country . . ."

People emerged onto the street. He saw familiar faces and
some new ones. If any were shouting this time, he could not hear
them above his own broadcast words.

"I also have things to teach you concerning the alternation of
crops, the use of fertilizers and superior irrigation techniques. The
water levels here have always been something of a problem, so I
have set up a demonstration of how this can be controlled by installing a series of automatic flow-control gates along the ditches
at the abandoned Branson farm above the west bend of the river.
I want you to go and take a look at this—to see how they work
all by themselves—after you have had a chance to think over my
words. No demons there either."

Stones and pieces of dirt and dung had begun striking the vehicle while he spoke, but these rebounded harmlessly and he continued:

"I have also fertilized, plowed, tilled and seeded one of the old fields there. I want you to see how smoothly and evenly this was done, and I want you to watch and see what the yield from that plot comes to. I believe that you will be impressed . . ."

Four men rushed forward and set hands upon the side of the car. They immediately leaped or fell back.

"That was an electrical shock," he stated. "I am not foolish enough to give you the same opportunity to harm me twice. Damn it! We're neighbors, and I want to help you! I want my town to be the center from which the entire country receives the benefits I wish to bring it! I have amazing things to teach you! This is only the beginning! Life is going to be better for everyone! I can build machines that fly and that travel under water! I can build weapons with which we can win any war! I have an army of mechanical servants! I—"

The pelting had become a steady hail, and larger, heavier objects were now falling.

"All right! I'm going!" he cried. "All that I want you to do is to think about the things that I have said! They may seem a lot more reasonable later, when you have cooled off! Go and look at the Branson place! I'll be back another time, when we can talk!"

The vehicle moved slowly forward. A few people chased after for a time, hurling some final rocks and words. Then they fell behind. He left the village.

As he swung to the left, climbing, about the side of a small hill, he saw a slim figure in a blue blouse and gray skirt, standing by the side of the trail, waving to him. He slowed immediately when he recognized Nora.

Coming to a stop, he leaned over and opened the door.

"Get in," he said.

She studied the car through narrowed eyes, then shook her head slowly.

"No," she said. "I thought you'd come this way, and I came on ahead to warn you—not to go for a ride in the thing."

"Warn me?"

"They're angry—"

"I know that."

She struck her fist against her palm.

"Don't interrupt! Listen! Could you hear what they were saying?"

"No. I—"

"I didn't think so, over all that noise. Well, I could, and I don't think that they are going to calm down and see things your way. I think that the only reason you're alive right now is that they couldn't break into this thing . . ." Gingerly, she reached out and touched the door. "Don't go back to the village. You probably ought to leave again—" Her voice broke and she turned away. "You never got in touch," she managed later. "You said that you would, and you never did."

"I— I couldn't, Nora."

"Where were you?"

"Far away . . ."

"Far? As far as Anvil Mountain, or one of the other forbidden places? That's where you got this thing, isn't it?"

He did not reply.

"Isn't it?" she repeated.

"It's not the way you think," he answered then. "Yes, I was there, but—"

"Go away! I don't want to know you any more! I've warned you. If you value your life, leave here again—and this time, don't come back!"

"I can convince you you're wrong—if you'll listen, if you will let me show you some—"

"I don't want to listen and I don't want to see anything!"

She turned and ran off through the trees. He would have pursued her, but he feared leaving the car there, should any villagers be following.

"Come back!" he called.

But there was no answer.

Reluctantly, he closed the door and continued on. A puzzled centaur peered after him from the hilltop.

VII.

The synthetic caterpillars crisscrossed the streets of the reviving city, removing trash and rubble. Their superintendent, a short, wide-shouldered mutant with heavy brow-ridges, followed their slow progress, occasionally leaning upon his hooked driving-prod. The skies were sunny today, above the shining spires about which laborers clambered, building. Terraces were spreading under the care of a company of robot attendants. The steady throbbing of the restored factories filled the air as other-styled robots, flying machines, cars and weapons moved down the computerized assembly lines. Far below, a line of passing mutants genuflected as they passed the white-stone monument above the entranceway to the old teaching machine's quarters, which their leader had caused to be erected there and had designated as a shrine. Giant bird-like forms departed from and returned to flat-roofed buildings, moving into and out of their enormous patrol patterns. The superintendent uttered a cry, swung his goad and smiled. Life had been growing steadily better, ever since the arrival of the sun-crowned one, with his power over the Old Things. He hoped that the leader fared well on his latest quest. Later, he would visit the shrine to pray for this, and that they might spread the blessings of warmth at night and regular meals across the land. A virtuous feeling he could now afford possessed him as he swung the goad again.

* * *

Michael Chain, florid-faced, hair thinning now, sat across from Daniel in the small, quiet restaurant, trying to seem as if he were not studying his reactions. Dan, in turn, uncomfortable in his best suit, poked at his melting dessert and sipped his coffee, trying to seem as if he were not aware of the surreptitious scrutiny. Occasionally, his wrist throbbed and somewhere a dish shattered. Whenever this occurred, he would hastily apply the biofeedback technique he had learned to suppress it.

"The record isn't doing too well, eh?" Michael said.

Dan raised his eyes, shook his head.

"I seem to go over better in person," he replied. Then he shrugged. "Hard to tell what you're doing wrong the first time around, though. I can already see a number of things I should have done differently—"

"It was good," Michael surprised him by saying. "I liked it." He flipped a palm upward and gestured vaguely away. "Even so," he went on. "A small outfit, no promotion . . . Do you have any idea how many songs are recorded each year?"

"Yes, I do. It's—"

". . . And you know something about statistics, even with a liberal arts background. It's practically a lottery situation."

"It's rough," Dan acknowledged.

The hand turned over and struck the tabletop.

"It's damn near impossible to make it, that's what it is."

A sound of breaking crockery emerged from the kitchen. Dan sighed.

"I suppose you're right, but I'm not ready to give it up yet."

The elder Chain called for an after dinner drink. Dan declined one.

"Still seeing that Lewis girl?"

"Yes."

"She strikes me as kind of cheap."

"We've had some good times together."

Michael shrugged.

"It's your life."

Dan finished his coffee. When he looked up, Michael was staring at him, smiling.

"It is," the older man said. He reached out and touched Dan's hand. "I'm glad your mind's your own. I know I sometimes push hard. But listen. Even without the degree, there'll always be a place for you in the firm. If you should ever change your mind, you can learn what you need on the job—pick up some night courses . . . No sales pitch. I'm just telling you. There'll still be a place."

"Thanks, Dad."

Michael finished his drink and looked about.

"Waiter!" he called. "The check!"

The chandelier began to quiver, but Dan recognized the feeling and quelled it in time.

* * *

Mor stood, leaning against the bedpost for support. He inserted a knuckle into an eyesocket and rubbed vigorously. It seemed that all he did these days was sleep. And his ankles, swollen again . . .

He raised the water bottle from the bedside table and took a long drink. He coughed, then swallowed a potion he had left ready, washing it down with another gulp of water.

Crossing the chamber, he drew back the long, dark drape and opened a shutter. Stars sparkled in a pale sky. Was it morning or evening? He was not certain.

Stroking his white beard, he stared out across the hushed land, realizing that something other than physiology had troubled his slumber. He waited for the dream, the message, the feeling to recur, but it did not.

After a long while, he let the drape fall, not bothering to close the shutter. Perhaps if he returned to bed, it might come back to him . . . Yes, that seemed a good idea.

Shaking his head slowly, he retraced his steps across the room. Human bodies are so much trouble, he reflected.

An owl hooted several times. The mice scurried within the walls.

* * *

Deep beneath the ruin of Castle Rondoval, weighted by the heavy spell of sleep that filled the cavern, Moonbird, mightiest of the dragons, assumed a stiff, heraldic pose upon the floor and relaxed it with equal suddenness, his sigh moving like a warm wind across the forms of his mates. His spirit fled ghostly across the skies, passing the forms of giant, dark birds with bodies like sword metal at heights only his kind had once held. Invisible, he threatened, then attacked. The creatures passed along their ways, unaffected.

Raging in his impotence, Moonbird retreated to the dark places of sleep, narrowly missing a smaller form nearby as he tossed, his claws raking furrows along a stony ledge.

VIII.

Mark was not awakened by the distant cries. He slept on long after they had begun and was only aroused when a figure entered his shed, seized hold of his shoulder and shook him violently.

"Wake up! Please! Wake up!" came a sharp whisper.

"What—" he began, and he felt a hand cover his mouth.

"Keep your voice down! It's me—Nora. They'll get this one soon enough, just for good measure. You must flee!"

The hand came away from his face. He sat up and reached for his boots, began drawing them on.

"What are you talking about?" he asked. "What is happening?"

"I tried to get here in time to warn you, but they were too fast," she said. "I remembered you sometimes slept in this shed . . ."

He seized his swordbelt and buckled it on.

"I've weapons in the barn to stop anything," he said. "I wish I'd kept some here—"

"The barn is burning, too!"

"Too?"

"The house, the small stable and the two nearer sheds are also on fire."

He sprang to his feet.

"My father was in the house!"

She caught hold of his arm, but he shook her off and made for the door.

"Don't!" she said. "It's too late! Save yourself!"

He flung the door wide and saw that she had spoken the truth. The house blazed like a torch. Its roof had already caved in. A number of townfolk were headed in his direction, and a cry went up as they sighted him.

He took a step backward.

"Get out through the rear window," he whispered, "or they'll know you were here. Hurry!"

"You come, too!"

"Too late. They've spotted me. Go!"

He stepped out, shut the door behind him and drew his blade.

As they approached, faces dirt-streaked and sweaty in the firelight, he thought of his last sight of old Marakas, passed out on his pallet in the loft. Too late, too late . . .

Father, they will pay for this!

He moved forward to meet them. As he advanced, he saw that some of them were armed with other than makeshift weapons. Old blades—some that he might have forged himself—had been freshly oiled and honed. Several of these shone in the midst of the mob. He did not slow his pace.

"Murderers!" he cried. "My father was in there! You all knew him! He never hurt anyone! Damn you! All of you!"

There was no reply, nor did he expect one. He fell upon them, swinging his blade. The nearest man, Hyme the tanner, cried out and dropped to the ground, clutching at his opened belly. Mark swung again, and the butcher's brother screamed and bled. His next attack was parried by one of the blades, and a staff struck him upon the left shoulder. He beat down a thrust toward his chest and fell back, swinging his blade in a wide arc, severing an extended hand clutching a club.

Ashes fell about them, and a line of fire moved through the long grasses toward the orchard. The barn shuddered and a wall gave way, crashing and spraying sparks off to his left.

He was struck upon the chest by something hard-thrown. He staggered back, still swinging the blade. A staff caught him again, this time upon the thigh, and he stumbled. They were all about him then, kicking, pushing. His blade was wrenched from his grasp. Immediately, his hand moved to the bracelet upon his left wrist. He pressed several of the studs . . .

A blade was swinging toward his head. He twisted aside, felt it cut into his brow, slip lower . . .

He screamed and covered his face.

And another voice also carried above the cries of his attackers. Beyond the pain, behind the blood, he recognized Nora's near-hysterical shout: "You'll kill him! Stop it! Stop it!"

Someone kicked him again, but it was the last blow that he felt.

A frightened scream arose nearby, soon to be echoed by many others, as a dark form dropped from the sky and plunged into the midst of his assailants. Its wings were like twin scythes and its metal beak rose and fell among them.

Mark drew a deep breath and staggered to his feet, his body a network of pain, his left hand still covering that half of his face, blood trickling between the fingers, running down the arm, filming the bracelet toward which his right hand now moved.

A number of men lay still upon the ground, and the dark bird stalked those who stood . . .

His fingers danced across the metal band.

The bird-thing halted, drew back, hopped, beat with its wings, rose into the air, circled . . .

"You have decided your own fates," Mark cried hoarsely.

The bird descended, seized hold of him by the shoulders, bore him aloft. His left hand was now entirely red and seemed firmly fixed to his face.

"I give those of you who still stand your lives—for now—that memory of this night shall remain among you, that witnesses be available," he called down to them. "I shall return, and all shall be

done as I said it earlier in town—but you will be subjects, not partners in the enterprise. I curse you for this night's work!"

The bird picked up speed, gained altitude.

". . . Save for you, Nora," he shouted finally. "I will be back for you—never fear!"

He vanished into the sky above. The wounded moaned and the fires crackled. Countercurses followed him across the night. His blood was a small rain over fields he had once worked.

IX.

After knocking and waiting—several times—she had just about given up on his being at home. She had also tried the door and found it to be secured.

She was tired. It had been a long walk up to the place, after an absolutely horrible night. She leaned against the doorframe, eyes sparkling, but she simply did not feel like crying. She drew back her foot and kicked the door as hard as she could.

"Open up, damn you!" she cried, and she heard a click and the door swung inward.

Mor stood there, wearing a faded blue robe, blinking at the light.

"I thought I heard someone scratching," he said. "You seem familiar, but I don't—"

"Nora. Nora Vail," she told him, "from the east village. I'm sorry I—"

Mor brightened.

"I remember. But I thought you were just a little girl . . . Of course! Excuse me. It flies." He stepped back. "Come in. I was just making some tea. Don't mind the litter."

She followed him through one curiously furnished room and into another. There, he cleared a chair for her and turned his attention to a boiling pot.

"It's terrible . . ." she began.

"It will wait until tea is ready," he said sternly. "I do not like terrible things on an empty stomach."

Nodding, she seated herself. She watched the old sorcerer, as he put out bread and preserves, as he brewed the tea. There was a trembling in his hands. His face, always deeply lined, was now unnaturally pallid. He had been correct, though, in that he had not seen her for years—she had been but a small girl when he had last stopped by for dinner, on his way to or from someplace. She recalled a surprisingly long conversation . . .

"There," he said, setting a plate and a cup on the table beside her. "Refresh yourself."

"Thank you."

Partway through the meal, she began talking. The story poured out in disjointed fashion, but Mor did not interrupt her. When she looked at him, she realized that some color had returned to his cheeks and the hand that held his cup seemed steadier.

"Yes, it is serious," he agreed when she had finished. "You were right to come to me. In fact—"

He rose and slowly crossed the chamber to stand before a small, dark mirror set within an iron frame.

"—I had best look into it immediately," he finished, and he passed his fingertips near the glass and muttered softly.

His back was to her and his right shoulder partly blocked her view of the glass, but she saw images dance within the exposed portions, and something like a section of a strange skyline appeared in the upper right quadrant, a vaguely disturbing silhouette circling above it. The entire prospect seemed to rush forward then, and she could not tell what it was that Mor was now regarding. Changes in lighting seemed to indicate several more scene shiftings after that, but she could not distinguish the details of subsequent images.

Finally, Mor moved his hands once again, across the face of it. All action fled, and darkness filled the glass like poured ink.

Mor turned away and moved back to his seat. He raised his teacup, sipped, made a face and dashed its tepid contents into the fire. He rose and prepared fresh tea.

"Yes," he repeated when he had returned and served them. "It is very serious. Something will have to be done about him . . ."

"What?" she asked.

He sighed.

"I do not know."

"But could not you, who banished the demons of Det—"

"Once," he said, "I could have stopped this changeling easily. Now, though . . . Now the power is no longer in me as it was in the old days. It is—too late for me. Yet, I am responsible in this."

"You? How? What do you mean?"

"Mark is not of this world. I brought him here as a babe, after the last great battle. He was the means whereby I exiled Pol Det-

son, the last Lord of Rondoval, also then a child. It is a strange
feeling—knowing that the man we got in exchange is now a far
greater menace than anything we had feared. I am responsible. I
must do something. But what, I cannot say."

"Is there someone you could ask for help?"

He touched her hand.

"I must be alone now—to think," he said. "Return to your
home. I am sorry, but I cannot ask you to remain."

She began to rise.

"There must be *something* you can do."

He smiled faintly.

"Possibly. But first I must investigate."

"He said that he would come back for me," she persisted. "I do
not want him to. I am afraid of him."

"I will see what can be done."

He rose and accompanied her to the door. On the threshold,
she turned impulsively and seized his hand in both of hers.

"Please," she said.

He reached out with his other hand and stroked her hair. He
drew her to him for a moment, then pushed her away.

"Go now," he said, and she did.

He watched until she was out of sight amid the greenery of the
trail. His eyes moved for a moment to a patch of flowers, a butterfly darting among them. Then he closed and barred the door
and moved to his inner chamber, where he mixed himself powerful medicines.

He took a quarter of the dosage he had prepared, then returned
to the room where he had sat with Nora.

Standing before the iron-framed mirror once again, he repeated
some of his earlier gestures above its surface, as well as several additional ones. His voice was firmer as he intoned the words of
power.

Some of the darkness fled the mirror, to reveal a dim room
where people sat at small tables, drinking. A young man with a
white streak through his hair sat upon a high stool on a platform
at the room's corner, playing upon a musical instrument. Mor

studied him for a long while, reached some decision, then spoke another word.

The scene shifted to the club's exterior, and Mor regarded the face of the building with almost equal intensity.

He spoke another word, and the building dwindled, retreating down the street as Mor watched through narrowed eyes.

He gestured and spoke once again, and the glass grew dark.

Turning away, he moved to the inner chamber, where he decanted the balance of the medicine into a small vial and fetched his dusty staff from the corner where he had placed it the previous summer.

Moving to a cleared space, he turned around three times and raised the staff before him. He smiled grimly then as its tip began to glow.

Slowly, he began pacing, turning his head from side to side, as if seeking a gossamer strand adrift in the air . . .

X.

Dan turned up his collar as he left the club, glancing down the street as he moved into the night. Cars passed, but there were no other pedestrians in sight. Guitar case at his side, he began walking in the direction of Betty's apartment.

Fumes rose through a grating beside the curb, spreading a mildly noxious odor across his way. He hurried by. From somewhere across town came the sound of a siren.

It was a peculiar feeling that had come over him earlier in the evening—as if he had, for a brief while, been the subject of an intense scrutiny. Though he had quickly surveyed all of the club's patrons, none of them presented such a heavy attitude of attention. Thinking back, he had recalled other occasions when he had felt so observed. There seemed no correlation with anything but a warm sensation over his birthmark—which was what had recalled the entire matter to him: he was suddenly feeling it again.

He halted, looking up and down the street, studying passing cars. Nothing. Yet . . .

It was stronger now than it had been back at the club. Much stronger. It was as though an invisible observer stood right beside him . . .

He began walking again, quickening his pace as he neared the center of the block, moving away from the corner light. He began to perspire, fighting down a powerful urge to break into a run.

To his right, within a doorway—a movement!

His muscles tensed as the figure came forward. He saw that it bore a big stick . . .

"Pardon me," came a gentle voice, "but I'm not well. May I walk a distance with you?"

He saw that it was an old man in a strange garment.

"Why . . . Yes. What's the matter?"

The man shook his head.

"Just the weight of years. Many of them."

He fell into step beside Dan, who shifted his guitar case to his left hand.

"I mean, do you need a doctor?"

"No."

They moved toward the next intersection. Out of the corner of his eye, Dan saw a tired, lined face.

"Rather late to be taking a walk," he commented. "Me, I'm just getting off work."

"I know."

"You do? You know me?"

Something like a thread seemed to drift by, golden in color, and catch onto the end of the old man's stick. The stick twitched slightly and the thread grew taut and began to thicken, to shine.

"Yes. You are called Daniel Chain—"

The world seemed to have split about them, into wavering halves—right and left of the widening beam of light the string had become. Dan turned to stare.

"—but it is not your name," the man said.

The beam widened and extended itself downward as well as forward. It seemed they trod a golden sidewalk now, and the street and the buildings and the night became two-dimensional panoramas at either hand, wavering, folding, fading.

"What is happening?" he asked.

"—and that is not your world," the man finished.

"I do not understand."

"Of course not. And I lack the time to give you a full explanation. I am sorry for this. But I brought you this way years ago and exchanged you for the baby who would have become the real Daniel Chain. You would have lived out your life in that place we just departed, and he in the other, to which you now must go. There, he is called Mark Marakson, and he has become very dangerous."

"Are you trying to tell me that that is my real name?" Dan asked.

"No. You are Pol Detson."

They stood upon a wide, golden roadway, a band of stars above them, a haze of realities at either side. Tiny rushes of sparks fled along the road's surface and a thin, green line seemed traced upon it.

"I fail to follow you. Completely."

"Just listen. Do not ask questions. Your life does depend upon it, and so do many others. You must go home. There is trouble in your land, and you possess a power that will be needed there."

Dan felt constrained to listen. This man had some power himself. The evidence of it lay all about him. And his manner, as well as his words, compelled attention.

"Follow that green line," the man instructed him. "This road will branch many times before you reach your destination. There will be interesting sideways, fascinating sights, possibly even other travelers of the most peculiar sort. You may look, but do not stray. Follow the line. It will take you home. I— Wait."

The old man rested his weight upon his staff, breathing deeply.

"The strain has been great," he said. "Excuse me. I require medication."

He produced a small vial from a pouch at his waist and gulped its contents.

"Lean forward," he said, moments later.

Dan inclined his head, his shoulders. The staff came forward, issuing a blue nimbus which settled upon him and seemed to sink, warmly, within his skull. His thoughts danced wildly, and for a long moment he seemed trapped in the midst of an invisible crowd, everyone babbling without letup about him.

"The language of that place," the man told him. "It will take awhile to sink in, but you have it now. You will speak slowly at first, but you will understand. Facility will follow shortly."

"Who are you? What are you?" Dan asked.

"My name is Mor, and the time has come for me to leave you to follow that line. There has to be an exchange of approximately equivalent living mass if the transfer is to be permanent. I must depart before I lose one of the qualifications. Walk on! Find your own answers!"

Mor turned with surprising energy and vanished into the rippling prospect to the right, as if passing behind a curtain. Dan took a step after him and halted. The shifting montage that he faced was frightening, almost maddening to behold for too long. He transferred his gaze back to the road. The green line was steady beneath the miniature storms.

He looked behind and saw that the glittering way seemed much the same as it did before him. He took one step, then another, following the green line forward. There was nothing else for him to do.

As he walked, he tried to understand the things that Mor had told him. What power? What menace? What changeling stepbrother? And what was expected of him at the green line's end? Soon, he gave up. His head was still buzzing from the onslaught of voices. He wondered what Betty would think when he failed to show up at her place, what his father would feel at his disappearance.

He halted and gasped. It only just then reached the level of realization that if this strange story were true, then Michael was not his father.

His wrist throbbed and a small, golden whirlwind rose, to follow him, dog-like, for several paces.

CHANGELING

He shifted the guitar case to his other hand and continued walking. As he did, he was taken by a small pattern in the mosaic ahead and to his left—a tiny, bright scene at which he stared. As he focussed his attention upon it, it grew larger, coming to dominate that entire field of vision, beginning to assume a three-dimensional quality.

Coming abreast of it, he saw that it had receded without losing any of its distinction. A side road now led directly toward it, and he realized that he could walk there in a matter of minutes.

He saw bright green creatures playing within a sparkling lake, blue mountains behind them, orange stands of stone rising from the water, serving as platforms upon which they rested and cavorted before diving back in again, brilliant sunlight playing over the entire prospect, giant red dragonflies wheeling and dipping above the lake's surface with amazing delicacy of motion, floating flowers, like pale, six-pointed stars . . .

He found his feet moving in that direction. The call of the place grew stronger . . .

Something yellow-eyed, long-eared and silver-furred passed him on the right, running bipedally, nose twitching.

"Late again!" it seemed to say. "Holy shit! She'll have my head, sure!"

It looked at him for an instant as it went by, its glance sliding past him along the way to the lake-scene.

"Don't go there!" it seemed to yell after him. "They eat warmbloods alive!"

He halted and shuddered. He looked away from the lake and its denizens, sought the green line, located it, returned there. By then, his informant was out of sight.

He tried to keep his eyes on the line as he continued, avoiding the sideshows as much as possible. It took an unexpected turn after a dozen paces, and he felt as if he were moving downhill for a time. Something like a red skateboard, bearing a large green scarab beetle, streaked by him. From time to time, he seemed to hear a chorus of voices singing something he could not distinguish.

He walked down this branch, and a piece of the action to his right seemed to beckon after his gaze. This time, he resisted, only to discover that the green line curved in that direction. A side road grew there as he advanced, and it seemed to lead on toward a forest.

The downhill sensation continued, and a breeze seemed to be blowing toward him. It smelled of leafmold and earth and flowering things. He hurried, and the scene moved toward him at more than a reciprocal pace. The tiny storms began to diminish underfoot, the green line was widening . . .

Suddenly, he heard bird-notes. He reached out and touched a treetrunk. The green line lost itself amid grasses. The world widened into a single place of forest and glade. The stars went out overhead, to be replaced by blue sky and clouds, crisscrossed by leafy boughs. He looked behind him. There was no road—only, for a moment, what seemed a golden strand of webbing, tossed by the wind toward his right, gone.

He began walking across the glade. Abruptly, he halted. He could wander lost for a long while if this were a sizable wood, and he had a feeling that it might be.

He removed his jacket, as the day was pleasant enough, placed it upon the trunk of a fallen tree, hoisted himself up and sat upon it. Better to stay right where he was until some plan of action suggested itself. This spot might in some way be significant as the terminus of his peculiar journey.

He opened the case to check on his guitar, which seemed intact. He raised it and began strumming upon it as he thought. It sounded all right, too.

He might locate a tree that looked more climbable than the giants which surrounded him, he decided, and see whether he could spot a town or a road from higher up. He looked about, without breaking his rhythm. Yes. That appeared to be a good one, a few hundred meters right rear . . . He faced forward again and almost missed a beat.

The tiny creature which cavorted before him looked exactly like what it was—a centaur colt. Its small hands moved in time with the rhythm, and it pranced.

Fascinated, he turned his attention to what he was playing,

switching to a more complicated righthand style. Softly, he began singing. His wristmark grew warm, throbbed. Shortly, two more of the small creatures emerged from the woods, to join the dancer. As a number of leaves blew by, as he felt they must—as he had half-consciously willed it—he caught these in the net of his playing and swirled them about the laughing child-faces, the rearing pony-bodies. He drew birds to spin after them, and a deer he had somehow known was present to join in the movements which were now taking on a pattern. The day seemed to darken, as he willed it—though it must only have been a cloud passing over the sun—to transform the spectacle into a twilit scene, which somehow struck him as most appropriate.

He played tune after tune, and other creatures came to join in —bounding rabbits, racing squirrels—and somehow he knew that this was right and proper, exactly as it should be, in this place, with him playing, now . . . He felt as if he might go on forever, building walls of sound and toppling them, dancing in his heart, singing . . .

He did not become aware of the girl until sometime after her arrival. Slim and fair, clad in blue, she appeared beside a tree, far to the left of the clearing, and stood beneath it, unmoving, watching and listening.

When he did notice her, he nodded, smiled and watched for her reaction. He wished to take no chance of frightening her away, making no sudden movements. When she returned his nod, with a small smile of her own, he stopped playing and placed the instrument back in its case.

The leaves fell, the animals froze for an instant then tore off into the woods. The day brightened.

"Hello," he ventured. "You live around here?"

She nodded.

"I was walking the trail back to my village when I heard you. That was quite beautiful. What do you call that instrument? Is it magic?"

"A guitar," he answered, "and sometimes I think so. My name is Dan. What's yours?"

"Nora," she said. "You're a stranger. Where are you from? Where are you going?"

He snapped the case shut and climbed down to the ground.

"I've come a great distance," he said slowly, seeking the proper sentence patterns, locating words with some hesitation, "just wandering, seeing things. I'd like to see your village."

"You are a minstrel? You play for your keep?"

He hauled down his coat and shook it out, draped it over his arm.

"Yes," he said. "Know anybody who needs one?"

"Maybe . . . later," she said.

"What do you mean?"

"There have been a number of deaths. No one will be in a festive mood."

"I am sorry to hear that. Perhaps I can find some other employment for a time, while I learn something of this land."

She brightened.

"Yes. I am sure that you could—now."

He picked up the guitar case and moved forward.

"Show me the way," he said.

"All right." She turned and he followed her. "Tell me about your homeland and some of the places you've been."

Best to make something up, he decided, something simple and rural. No telling yet what things are like here. Better yet, get her to talking. Hate to start out sounding like a liar . . .

"Oh, one place is pretty much like another," he began. "Is this farming country?"

"Yes."

"Well, there you are. So is mine. What sorts of crops do you grow?"

They came to the trail and she led him downward along it. Whenever a bird passed overhead, she looked upward and flinched. After a time, he found himself scanning the skies, also. He was able to direct the conversation all the way into town. By the time they got there, he had learned the story of Mark Marakson.

XI.

The old man in the faded blue robe walked the streets of the drowsing city, past darkened storefronts, parked vehicles, spilled trashcans, graffiti that he could not read. His step was slow, his breathing heavy. Periodically, he paused to lean upon his staff or rest against the side of a building.

Slowly, light began to leak through the dark skyline before him, a yellow wave, rising, putting out stars. Far ahead, a shadowy oasis beckoned: trees, stirred by the faintest of morning breezes down a wide thoroughfare.

His stick tapped upon the concrete, more heavily now, as he crossed a sidestreet and negotiated another block with faltering steps. His hand trembled as he reached out to grasp a lamppost. Several vehicles passed as he stood swaying there. When the street was clear, he crossed.

Nearer. It was nearer now, the place where the boughs swayed and the songs of birds rose in the early morning light. He strode clumsily ahead, the faintest of blue flickers occasionally dancing at the tip of his stick. The breeze brought him a weak, flower-like aroma as he bore toward the final corner.

He rested again, breathing heavily, almost gasping now. When he moved to cross this street, his gait was stiff, awkward. Once he fell, but there was no traffic and he recovered and staggered on.

The sky had grown pink beyond the small park which now lay before him. His staff, from which the final light had faded, swung clumsily through a patch of flowers which closed immediately, undisturbed, behind it. He did not hear the faint hiss of the aerosols as he crossed the fake grass to slump against the bole of a standard model midtown park area tree, but only breathed the fragrance he had hoped might be there, smiling faintly as the breezes bore it to him, eyes following the dance of the butterflies in the still fresh light of the new-risen sun.

His staff slipped from his fingers and his breath came short and rushed as unnumbered mornings past joined with this one to smear all colors and smells into a greater reality which finally told the story he had always wondered at, through to its vision past objects. One of the butterflies, passing too near on its beam, was overtaken by his life's final throb, to settle, fluttering, upon his upturned wrist near to the dragonmark it bore.

With a blare and a rattle, the city came alive about him.

XII.

Strange feelings came and went. Each time that they came they were a little stronger; each time they departed some residuum remained. It was difficult to pin them down, Dan thought, as he drove a peg into a fencepost, but perhaps they had something to do with the land itself—this place that felt so familiar, so congruent to his tastes . . .

A cow strayed near, as if to inspect his work.

No, go that way, he willed. *Over there,* and his wrist felt warm, as with power overflowing, spilling from his fingertips, and the cow obeyed his unspoken command.

. . . Like that, he decided. It feels right, and I get better at it all the time.

A peg shattered under a hammer blow and a splinter flew toward his face.

Away! he commanded, without thinking.

Reflex-like, something within him moved to stop it, and the fragment sped off to the right.

. . . And like that.

He smiled as he finished the work and began collecting his tools. Shadows were growing across the pasture as he looked back along the lengths of fencing he had repaired. It was time to wash, to get ready for the dinner, the performance.

For three days now he had stayed at Nora's uncle's place, sleeping in the barn, turning his hand to odd jobs the old man had been unable to get to. In that time, his familiarity with the language had grown, just as Mor had said it would, almost as if he were remembering . . .

Mor . . . He had not thought of him for a time. It was as if his mind had locked away the entire experience of his journey to this place in some separate, off-limits compartment. It was just too bizarre, despite the fact that he walked where he now walked. But now, the effects of distancing made him cast back, examining that magical walk, wondering how his absence was being taken in his own world. He was surprised to find that his own past, now, was beginning to feel dream-like and unreal. Whereas this land . . .

He drew a deep breath. This was real, and somehow it felt like home. It would be good to meet more of the neighbors.

As he cleaned the tools and stored them in their places, he thought about the evening's steer roast at the field in toward town. Real country living, this, and he was enjoying it. He could think of worse places to be stuck for life. And afterwards, of course, he would play for them . . . He had been itching to get his hands on his guitar all day. There seemed peculiar new effects —paramusical, as it were—that he could manage in this place, and he wanted to experiment further. He wanted to show these things off, for the neighbors, for Nora . . .

Nora. He smiled again as he stripped off the heavy workshirt belonging to her Uncle Dar and walked back to bathe in the creek before donning his own garments. She was a pretty little thing. It was a shame to see her so frightened by the local inventor of a few mechanical toys . . .

And if this—Mark Marakson—were indeed Michael's son . . . He could almost see some genetic factor operating both in the aptitudes and the total lack of appreciation for possible reactions to their operation. Too bad he wasn't back home and in the business. He and Michael would probably have gotten along well.

But, as he washed the sweat and dust from his body, another thought came to trouble him. Why was he here? Mor had spoken with some urgency, as if his presence were a necessary thing. For what? Something involving Mark's creations. He snorted. It did seem to have been something of the sort, mentioned only in the vaguest of terms. But what mechanical menace could a society this simple turn out in a single generation? And why call upon *him* to combat it? No. He felt underinformed and the subject of an enigmatic old man's alarmist fantasies. But he did not feel victimized. When he got his bearings, he would learn more about this place, though he already felt it to be in many ways preferable to the society from which he had strayed. Why, he might yet become a genuine minstrel . . .

He dried himself with a piece of rough sacking and donned the loose, long-sleeved white shirt he had worn upon his arrival. He

changed back into his black denim trousers, but retained the
boots he had been given. They fit him well and seemed func-
tionally superior to the shoes he had worn on his hike between
the worlds.

He combed his hair, cleaned his fingernails and grinned at his
reflection in the water. Time to get his guitar and meet Nora and
her uncle. Things were looking up. He whistled as he walked
back toward the house.

There were bonfires and lanterns casting impressive shadows.
The remains of feasting were even now being gathered up from
about the field. At first, Dan felt as if he should not have had
those extra glasses of wine, and then he felt that he should have.
Why not? It was a festive occasion. He had met a great number
of the villagers, anxious for some diversion after the unpleasant
events of several days past, and he had succeeded with some
grace in parrying questions concerning his homeland. Now he was
ready to perform.

He dallied a little longer, until the bustle had ceased and people began seating themselves about the low hill he was to occupy.
The lanterns were moved nearer, encircling it.

He made his way forward then, breaking the circle, mounting
the rise, the instrument case a familiar weight in his right hand.
There came a soft flutter of applause and he smiled. It was good
to feel welcome after only a few days in a new place.

When he reached the top, he removed the guitar from its case
and put on the strap. He tuned it quickly and started to play.

Partway through the first tune, he began feeling at ease. The
good mood grew within him as he played several more and began
singing in his own tongue. Then he attempted the first of a group
he had tried translating into theirs. It was well-received, and he
swung immediately into another.

Looking out over his audience, he could only distinguish the
expressions on the nearest faces—smiling or concentrating—in
the lantern light. The listeners farther back were partly hidden by
shadows, but he assumed similar attention from their immobility,

from their joining in the applause whenever he rested. He saw Nora off to the left, seated near her uncle, smiling.

He broke into a virtuoso number of his own composition, a rousing piece which kept increasing in tempo. He suddenly wanted to show off. He rocked back and forth as he played. A breeze tousled his hair, rippled his garments . . .

It must not have been the first gasp, which reached him during the first lull. He would not have heard any earlier exclamation over his playing. But there were also murmurs, where before there had been only applause or silent attention. There came an indistinguishable cry from the back of the audience. He looked all about, attempting to ascertain its cause.

Then, "Devil!" he heard distinctly from nearby, and something dark flew past his head.

"The mark! The mark!" he now heard, and a stone struck him on the shoulder.

"Dragonmark!"

He realized that his right sleeve had been drawn back almost to his elbow during the last number, exposing his birthmark. But still, why should it cause such alarm?

"Detson!"

A shock went through him at that last word. He instantly recalled old Mor's telling him that his name was actually Pol Detson. But—

The next stone struck him on the forehead. He dropped the guitar into the case and snapped it shut, to protect it. Another stone struck him. The crowd was on its feet.

He felt a terrible anger rise within him, and his wrist throbbed as it never had before. Blood was running down his brow. His chest was sharply struck by another cast stone.

He stumbled as he attempted to raise the case and turn away. Something struck him on the neck, something sounded against the case's side . . .

The crowd had begun to move forward, past the lanterns, up the hill, slowly, stopping to grope for missiles.

Away! He was not aware whether he had shouted it or sounded

---

it only in his mind, accompanied by a broad, sweeping motion of his right arm.

People stumbled, fell, tripped over lanterns. All of the other lanterns seemed to topple spontaneously. There were dark shapes in the air, but none of them struck him. The grasses at the foot of the knoll began to take fire. The cries that now came up to him seemed less angry than frustrated, or frightened.

Away!

He gestured again, his entire arm tingling, a sensation of warmth flowing through his hand, out his fingertips. More people fell. The flames spread about them.

Clutching his guitar case, he turned and fled down the rear of the hill, leaping over sprawled forms and low fires, his breath al-

most a sob as he tore across the field, heading toward the dark
wood to the north.

The anger subsided and the fear grew as he ran. His last glance
back before he entered the trees seemed to show him the beginnings of pursuit. Supposing they fetched horses? They knew their
own country and he had no idea where he was headed. There
might be all sorts of places where they could cut him off, and
then—

Why? he wondered again, dodging about trees, crashing
through underbrush, wiping spiderwebs from his face, blood from
his eyes. Why had they suddenly turned on him when they had
seen the mark? What could it mean to them?

After stumbling for the third or fourth time, he halted and
stood panting, resting his back against the bole of a large tree. He
could not be certain how near his pursuers might be, unable to
distinguish other sounds over his breathing and the heavy beating
of his heart. But this wild rushing was doing him no good. He
was hastening exhaustion in addition to leaving a well-defined
trail. To move cautiously, to expend his energies more economi-
cally . . . Yes. He would have to proceed differently.

Mor had addressed him as the possessor of some power, and he
was not blind to the fact that he had just exercised it in a wild
fashion in escaping. Back home, save for mainly playful inter-
ludes in smoky, late-night clubs, he had always striven to suppress it, to keep it under control. Here, though, he already had
the name of witch or wizard, and if there were some way that that
power could serve him further, he was ready to learn it, to use it
to the confusion of his enemies.

His thoughts turned to the obvious connection, the mark upon
his wrist, as his breathing became more even. Immediately, he felt
the warmth and the heightened sense of his pulsebeat.

He continued to dwell upon it in his mind. What is it,
specifically, that I need? he wondered.

A safe way out of here, to a place of safety, he decided. The
ability to see where I am going and not run into things . . .

As he attempted to order this, he felt the forces within him stir, then saw the dragonmark clearly, despite the darkness. It seemed to move, brightening, then drift away from his arm to hover in the air before him, glowing faintly.

It passed slowly to the left and he followed it, its pale light dimly but surely illuminating his way. He lost all track of time as he pursued its passage through the forest. Twice, it halted, when he realized how tired he had become. On these occasions, he rested—once, beside a stream, where he drank deeply.

He remembered very few details of that long first night of his flight, save that at some point he realized that his way had taken a turn uphill and that this remained his course until light began to seep through the leaves overhead. With this, a sense of fatigue and time passed came over him, and he began casting about for a place to sleep. Immediately, his firefly dragon veered to the right, heading downhill for what must have been the first time in hours.

It led him among a maze of boulders to a small, rock-shielded dell, and there it hovered. Accepting the omen, he sprawled in the grass. From somewhere nearby, there came the sound and smell of running water.

He felt asleep almost immediately.

When he awakened, it was late in the day. His ghostly guide was gone, he ached in a number of places and he was hungry.

The first thing that he did was to remove his guitar from its case and inspect it for damage. He found that it had come through the night's ordeal intact. Then he sought the water—a small stream, a hundred or so meters to the right of the rocks—where he stripped and bathed and cleaned his wounds. The water was too chill for comfort, so he did not dally there. The sun was already falling fast, and he felt he could continue in relative safety.

Continue? At what point had his flight become a journey? He was not certain. Possibly while he slept. For it did feel now that his glowing guide had been doing more than helping him escape the villagers. Now he felt, intuitively—certainly not logically— that there was a definite destination ahead for him, that his will-o'-the-wisp had been guiding him toward it. He decided to let it continue on, if it would, though first it would be nice to find some food . . .

He repeated the process which had summoned the guide, and it came again, paler in this greater light, but sufficiently distinct to direct his course. As he followed it, he wondered whether it would be visible to another person.

It led him downhill for a time, and a little after sunset he found himself in the midst of a large orchard. He gorged himself and filled his pockets and all the odd nooks in the guitar case.

The guide led him uphill after that, and sometime during the middle of the night the trees grew smaller and he realized—looking back by moonlight—that had it been daytime, he could have seen for a great distance.

Before much longer, the way steepened, but not before he had caught a glimpse of a large building on a crest ahead. It was not illuminated and it appeared to be partly in ruin, but he had a premonition the moment that he saw it, reinforced by the behavior of the dragon-light. For the first time, the light appeared as if it were trying to hurry him along the trail.

He allowed himself to be hurried. An excitement was rising in his breast, accompanied by an unexplainable feeling that ahead lay safety—as well as shelter, food, warmth—and something else, something undefined and possibly more important than any of the others. He shifted his guitar case to his other hand, squared his shoulders and ignored his aching feet. He even forgot to wish again for the coat he had left behind, when a chill wind came down from the height and embraced him.

                              *   *   *

He would have liked to wander about the wrecked hall, surveying some of the more picturesque destruction, but the light pressed steadily ahead, leading him along a back corridor and into what could only be a pantry. The food stored all about him looked as fresh as if it had just been brought in. He reached im-

mediately toward a loaf of bread and stopped, puzzled, his hand
blocked by an invisible barrier.

No . . . Not quite invisible. For as he stared, he slowly became
aware of a mesh of softly pulsing blue strands which covered everything edible.

A preservation spell, came into his mind, as though he had activated a mental recording. *Use the guide to solve it—selectively.*

He tried mentally calling upon the hovering image of his mark
for assistance. It drifted back and merged with the original one
upon his wrist, the light flowing outward, into his hand. Suddenly,
he felt a gentle tugging at it and relaxed and let it move through a
series of gestures which finally bore it forward into a gap now ap-
parent in the meshing.

He seized the bread; also, some meat and cheese that were
within reach. After he had withdrawn his hand for the final time,
he felt the tugging again. Again, he let himself be guided, and this
time he saw the gap close, returning to its initial state of taut web-
work.

On another shelf, he located some wine bottles and repeated
the performance to obtain one.

As he gathered together the meal, he felt a strong urge to
depart. He released the light and was pleased to see that it had a
route mapped out for him. It led him up a flight of stairs and into
a chaotic room which once might have been a library.

He cleared a place on the writing desk and set down his
supplies. Then, by dint of intense concentration, he was able to
cause his drifting light to hover, successively, over the end of
each taper in a heavy candelabrum which he had uprighted and
repaired, causing each to spring into flame. He seemed to grow
better at such heat-thinking with each effort.

When the room was thus more fully illuminated, he retired his
pale guide and seated himself to dine. He noted that the chamber
had indeed been a library, many of its books now in disarray
upon the floor. As he ate, he wondered whether Mor's language-
treatment had extended to the written word.

Finally, unable to contain himself any longer, he rose and retrieved a volume from the clutter. When he got it into the light,

he smiled. Yes, he could decipher the runic lettering. This one appeared to be a travel book—though in his world it would have passed for some sort of mythology text. It described the dwellings of harpies and centaurs, salamanders and feathered serpents, it showed pyramids and labyrinths and undersea caverns, accompanied by cautionary notes as to their denizens, natural and otherwise. In the margins were penned an occasional "Very true" or "Hogwash!"

As he read, Dan—Should he begin thinking of himself as "Pol" now? he had wondered earlier. Why not? he had finally decided. A new name for a new life . . .

As he read, Pol felt his attention being constantly drawn toward the middle shelf across the room to his left. At one point, he put down his book and stared at it. There was almost something there . . .

Finally, when he had finished eating, he rose and moved to inspect the shadowy section of shelving. As he did, three faint, red threads seemed to be fluttering at its rear. They were possessed of the same insubstantial quality as the blue ones in the pantry. Was this land—or this place, in particular—causing him to develop a kind of second sight?

He cleared the remaining books from the shelf and stacked them near his feet. Then, slowly, he extended his hand, waiting for a guiding impulse. His left hand trembled at his side. Two hands seemed required then, or just the left. Very well . . . He raised it and advanced it. Then the middle fingers of his left hand caught the lower thread between them and raised it. The index finger hooked the upper strand and drew it downward, twining the two. His right hand was then drawn forward, all fingers and the thumb bunching to seize the tip of the third thread, to wrap it three times counterclockwise about the twisted pair . . .

He drew the bunch down, released it and struck it twice with his left fist.

"Open. Open," he said.

The panel at the rear dropped forward, revealing a hidden compartment. He began to reach and recoiled instantly. There lay another spell, hidden, coiled like a smoky snake, an interesting knot at its tail, designed to trap the unwary. He smiled faintly. It was going to be an intriguing problem. The working out of the previous one had become something of a conscious process as he had labored over it, gaining some small understanding of the thought and effort that had gone into its casting. Moving his left hand cautiously crossbody, two fingers extended, he reached forward . . .

Later, he sat back at the desk, reading a history of the Castle Rondoval and its illustrious if somewhat eccentric inhabitants. Several volumes of personal observations on the Art were stacked before him, along with his father's journals and notebooks on sundry matters. He read through the entire night, however, before he realized his own connection with the inhabitants of the place. Light had already spilled into the world when he came across a reference to the dragon-shaped birthmark inside the right wrists of the children of Rondoval.

But this excitement spent the balance of his energy. Shortly, he began to yawn and could not stop. His garments became a heavy weight upon him. He cleared a couch at the room's far end, curled up upon it and was soon asleep, to dream that he wandered these halls in a state of full repair and more than a little glory.

* * *

During the next afternoon, he ate a large meal and later solved the spell for a sunken tub on the ground floor, bringing him water for a bath (diverted, it seemed, from a nearby river, though he could not understand the twisting of the yellow and orange threads which appeared to govern its temperature). He committed these things to memory as he filled and drained the pool repeatedly, scouring it for his use. Then he luxuriated for a long while, wondering how Rondoval had come to achieve its present state of decay, and what had become of the rest of the family.

As he wandered later, uprighting furniture, tossing trash out of windows, unscrambling and memorizing a number of minor

spells, he decided to return to the library for one of the secret books he had thumbed, which had partly mapped the place.

The books now returned to their shelves, the room dusted after a fashion, he poured a glass of wine and studied the materials before him. Yes, there were many drawings, a number of floorplans, sketches of the place at various moments in its history and one rough outline of a vast series of caverns below, across which someone had penned "The Beasts." He did not know whether to chuckle or shudder. Instead, in response to an unvoiced desire, a blue-green thread came drifting by him. He hooked it with the first joint of the little finger of his right hand, twined it three times about his glass, tugged upon it twice with his middle finger accompanied by the appropriate image-commands, untwined it and dismissed it. Yes, now it was properly chilled.

Rising, he placed the book in the pocket of the dark jacket he had found in a wardrobe earlier and dusted thoroughly when he saw that it fit him so well. He carried the wineglass with him as he walked out and descended the stair to the main floor. "Beasts," he said aloud, and smiled . . . Images of the villagers hurling stones through the night returned to him. "Beasts," he repeated, making his way to a small storeroom where he had discovered lanterns and fuel earlier.

Walking the dim tunnels, occasionally consulting his guidebook, the lantern in his left hand casting sharp-edged shadows upon the rough walls, he could almost smell the concentration of power ahead. Whenever he looked in that certain way, he could see great multicolored bunches of streamers in the air. Nowhere else had he yet witnessed signs of such massive workings. He had no idea what it represented, other than that it must be something of great importance. Nor had he any notion whether his newly awakened powers could have any effect whatsoever upon it. As he brushed his fingertips against the strands, it seemed almost as if he could feel the mumble of mighty words, echoing infinitely, slowly, along a vast convoluted circuit. If he tried very hard . . .

Several minutes later, he found his way barred by a huge slab of stone. Strands led around it, wrapped it, crisscrossed it. There had to be a spell involved, but he wondered whether he would also need a dozen men with prybars to dislodge it, once any magical booby-traps had been defused. He moved nearer, studying the pattern of the strands. There did seem something of a method to their positioning . . .

The strands faded as his eyes slipped back into more normal channels of perception. Then he saw what it was that had distracted him. He raised the lantern and moved nearer, to read the inscription he now beheld:

PASS AT YOUR PERIL. HERE SLEEP THE HORRORS OF RONDOVAL.

He chuckled. They may be horrors, he thought, but I'm going to need a little muscle in this world. So, by God! now they're *my* horrors!

He set down the lantern and shifted his attention back to the colored strands.

. . . Just like unwrapping a very peculiar present, he thought, reaching forward with both hands.

He felt the tangles of power and began the motions that would unlock them. As he worked, the subaural mumbling returned, growing, intensifying, until words burst into his consciousness and he cried them out at the same time, whipping his hands back from the final threads and taking three timed paces backwards: "Kwathad! . . . Melairt! . . . Deystard!"

The slab shuddered and began to topple away from him. He realized then that the spell must have been infinitely more difficult to lay than it had been to raise. All of that power had had to be channeled from somewhere and bound up here. His own work had been more on the order of figuring out how to pull a plug.

The crash that followed echoed and reechoed until he could not help but be impressed by the enormity of the cavern that must lie behind.

He had snatched up the lantern, covered half his face with his sleeve and squinted until the reverberations and the hail of stone chips had settled. Then he moved cautiously forward, crossing the cracked monolith he had toppled.

He was about to raise the lantern to look around the vast hall,

when his new key of vision registered an enormous collection of filaments, like a multicolored ball of string larger than himself, resting just off to his left. Individual strands departed it in all directions before him. He realized that it would have taken ages to work each separate spell and then, in some fashion, join them at this common center. No . . . It had to have been done the other way around . . . He could not yet conceive of the manner of its laying, but he'd a sudden flash of insight into its undoing. It, too, could fall like the door before his new skill.

However . . . Could he control whatever he released. A good man had obviously spent a lot of time and energy putting the thing together. Best to have a look around before doing anything else . . .

He raised the lantern.

Dragons, dragons, dragons . . . Acres of dragons and other fantastic beasts lay all about him, extending far beyond his feeble light. His eyes caught them at another level, also. To each of them extended one strand of the master spell.

He lowered the light. What the hell do you say to a dragon? How do you control one? He shuddered at the thought of releasing any of the slumbering horrors.

Probably wake up hungry, too . . .

He began to back away.

Clear out. Forget this part of the family heritage. They must have bred tougher Lords of Rondoval in the old days . . .

As he began to turn away, his attention was caught by a single green filament. Its color was slightly darker than any of the others, and it was also the thickest one in sight, almost twice the size of its mates. What might it tether? he wondered.

Suddenly, all the dreamlands he had ever read of or conjured in song, all the fantasy worlds he had ever sculpted of smoke or walked through at bedtime as a child rose before him, and he knew that he could not leave this place without looking upon the prodigy bound by this mighty spell. Turning back, he followed the strand among the massive sleepers, averting his eyes as well as his feet in some instances.

When he reached out to brush the strand with his fingertips, a

sound like a crystal bell echoed within his head, "Moonbird . . ."
—constantly fading—and he knew that to be the name of the
creature toward which he as headed.

"Moonbird," he said, fingers still feeling the pulse of the cord.

*Lord, I hear, beyond the depths of sleep or life. Shall we range
the skies together, as in days gone by?*

*I am not the lord you knew, and Rondoval has come upon sad
times,* he thought back, still brushing the cord.

*What matter? So long as there is a lord in Rondoval. You are
of the blood?*

Yes.

*Then call me back from these ghost skies. I'll bear you where
you would.*

I am not even sure I know what to feed you . . .

I'll manage, never fear.

. . . And then there is the problem of this spell.

Not for one such as—

Pol halted, for he could go no further. His hand had left the
strand awhile back, as it seemed tangled on an overhead ledge.
For several moments, he had thought it was a huge mineral formation which confronted him—a vast mound of scaly copper
bearing the green patina of age. But it had moved, slightly, as he
had watched.

He sucked air between his teeth as he raised the lantern. There,
there was the great crested head! How huge those eyes must be
when opened! He reached out and touched the neck. Cold, cold
as metal. Perhaps nearly as tough.

"How low must your fires now be, bird of the moon . . ." he
said.

Back to him came a jumbled vision of clouds and tiny houses,
forests like patches of weeds . . .

. . . Shall we range the skies together?

The fear was gone, leaving only a great desire to see the huge
beast freed.

He moved back to the first place where the strand came within
reach again. He touched it as he began to follow it back out.

Patience, father of dragons. We shall see . . .

. . . And kill your enemies.

First things first.

He followed it back to the ball of plaited rainbows near the entrance. He traced its point of entry into the mass and noted each place where it became visible again at the surface. Would it be possible to tease out this one strand? Could he arouse Moonbird without awakening all the others?

He stared for a long while before he moved, and then his first gestures were tentative. Soon, though, his left arm was plunged past the elbow into the glowing sphere, his fingers tracing each twisting of the thick, green strand . . .

Later, he stood holding it free, its end twisted about his finger. He walked quickly back, to stand regarding the drowsing giant once again.

Awaken now, he willed, untwining it, releasing it.

The thread drifted away, shriveling. The dragon stirred.

Even bigger than I thought, he decided, staring into the suddenly opened eye which now regarded him. Much bigger . . .

The mouth opened and closed in a swallowing movement, revealing spike-like ranks of teeth.

Those, too . . .

He moved nearer.

. . . Must seem bold for a little longer, establish where we both stand right away . . .

He reached out and laid his hand upon the broad neck.

I am Pol Detson, Lord of Rondoval until further notice, he tried to communicate.

The giant head was raised, turned, the mouth opened . . . Suddenly, the tongue shot forward, licking him with a surface the texture of a file, knocking him backwards.

. . . Master!

He recovered himself, dodged a second caress of the tongue and patted the neck again.

Contain yourself, Moonbird! I am—soft.

Sometimes I forget.

The dragon spread it wings and lowered them, drew itself upright, raised and lowered its head, nuzzled him.

Come, mount my back and let us fly!

Where?

Out the old tunnel, to view the world.

Pol hesitated, his courage ebbing.

. . . But if I don't do it now, I never will, he decided. I know that. Whereas, if I do, I may be able to do it again one day. And I may need to . . .

A moment, he communicated, looking for the easiest way up.

Moonbird lowered his head fully and extended his neck.

Come.

Pol mounted, located what he hoped was a traditional dragon rider's position, above the shoulders, at the widening base of the neck. He clung with his legs and his arms. Behind him, he heard the vanes stir.

I sense that you play a musical instrument, Moonbird began, as they moved forward (To distract him? No—too sophisticated a concept). *You must bring it next time and play to me as we fly, for I love music.*

That might be novel.

They sprang from the ground and Moonbird immediately located a draft of air which they followed into a broader, higher part of the cavern. The light from the lantern Pol had left on the ground dwindled quickly, and they flew through an absolute darkness for what seemed a long while.

Suddenly, with a rush of cool air, there were stars all about them. A moment later, surprising himself, Pol began to sing.

XIII.

Mark rolled out of his bed, drew the purple dressing gown about his shoulders and sat clutching his head, waiting for the room to stop spinning.

How long had it been—four, five, six days?—since the robosurgeon had worked him over?

He raised his head. The room was dark. The thing which protruded from his left eyesocket hummed. Finally, it grew silent and he had vision on that side.

He rose and crossed the meticulously well-kept chamber—all metal and plastic and glass—and regarded himself in the mirror above the washstand. He tapped lightly with his fingertips about the perimeter of the lens case, where it joined his brow and cheekbone.

. . . Still too tender. Impair efficiency to take too many drugs, but I'll need some more to be able to think at all . . .

He withdrew a container of tablets from a drawer in the stand, gulped two and proceeded to wash and shave without turning on a light.

. . . It does have some advantages, though, especially if you get turned around this way. Must be the middle of the night . . .

He drew on a pair of brown trousers with many pockets, a green sweater, a pair of boots. He opened the rear door of his apartment and stepped out onto the terrace. His personal flier stood on the pad—delta-winged, compact, glassy and light. Mechanical things rose and fell in the distance, some only visible in his left field of vision. He inhaled the fragrance of imported plants, turned, crossed to an elevator hatch, dropped three levels —to a footbridge leading across the road. He crossed there, heading for the surveillance center in the lower, adjacent building.

One of the small, gnarled men, clad in a brown and black uniform, sat before a bank of glowing screens. Whether he actually watched any of them was something Mark could not tell from the rear—one of the reasons he disliked using people except in situations such as this where he had no choice.

As he approached, his optic prosthesis hummed, its lens becoming a greenish color as it adjusted to the lighting. The man straightened in his chair.

"Good evening, sir," he said, not turning away from the screens.

. . . Damned sharp senses these fellows have.

"Anything to report?"

"Yes, sir. Two surveillance birds are missing."

"Missing? Where?"

"The village, your own—"

"What happened to them?"

"Don't know, sir. They just suddenly weren't there anymore."

"How long ago was this?"

"A little over three hours ago, sir."

"Didn't you try to maneuver any of the others to get a look at what was happening?"

"It was too sudden, sir."

"In other words, nothing was done. Why wasn't I notified immediately?"

"You had left orders not to be disturbed, sir."

"Yes . . . I know. What do you make of it?"

"No idea, sir."

"It has to be a malfunction of some sort. Pull back the others in that area for complete inspections. Send out fresh ones. Wait!"

He moved nearer and studied the appropriate screens.

"Any activity in the village?"

"None, sir."

"The girl has not been out of her house?"

"No, sir. It has been dark for hours."

"I think I may pick her up tomorrow. It depends on how I feel. Plan B, three birds—two for safety escort. See that they're standing ready."

"Yes, sir."

The small man stole a glance at him.

"I must say, sir. The new eye-thing is most attractive."

"Oh? Really? Thank you," he mumbled, then turned and left.

What had he been thinking? The pills must be starting to work . . . He wouldn't be in shape by tomorrow. Wait another day. Should he go back and countermand that last order? No. Let it stand. Let it stand . . .

He wandered down to spot-check a factory, his eye humming its way to yellow.

*　*　*

Lantern swinging, shadows bouncing from his rapid step, the small man passed along the maze of tunnels, occasionally pausing to listen and to peer about abrupt corners. Usually, when he halted, he also shuddered.

It might almost have been easier without the lantern, he thought, back there. And that slab . . . He did not remember that broken slab at the cave mouth.

He thought back upon the scene he had witnessed immediately after awakening. The man acting almost as if he were talking with that monster, then mounting it and flying off, fortunately leaving his lantern behind. Who could it have been, and what the circumstances?

He turned right at the next branching, remembering his way. There seemed to be no sounds, other than those of his own making. Rather peculiar, in the aftermath of such a battle . . .

When he finally reached the foot of the huge stair, he left the lantern. He moved soundlessly through the darkness, toward some small illumination above. When his eyes just cleared the top step, he halted and surveyed the hall.

"How long have I slept?" he asked of, perhaps, the tattered tapestry.

But he did not wait for a reply.

*   *   *

As the sun pinked the eastern corner of the sky, Moonbird descended slowly to land upon the last steady tower of Rondoval. Pol dismounted and slapped him upon the shoulder.

Good morrow, my friend. I will call you again soon.

I will hear. I will come.

The great dark form leapt from the tower and drifted across the sky, heading for one of the hidden entrances to the caverns. A green strand seemed to connect its shoulder to Pol's still upraised hand. It faded soon to join the other strands of the world, drifting everywhere.

For several moments, he watched the stars fading in the west, wondering at the strange flying things Moonbird had destroyed earlier, wondering even more at the beast's comment, *They had troubled my dreams.*

Turning, with a glance to the sunrise, he entered the tower, to make his way down and around within it, returning to the library which had come more and more to feel like home. He hummed as he walked, occasionally snapping his fingers. He finally felt that he belonged—a member of the magic-working, dragon-riding family which had lived here. He wanted to take his guitar into his hands and sing about it, watching the dust depart the surfaces in each chamber through which he strolled, the furniture move itself about, the debris roll into heaps in corners, the strands of power which controlled these operations attaching themselves to, reso-nating with, his instrument. Rondoval did actually feel more *his* at this moment than it had at any time before.

When he reached the library, he moved to pour himself a drink, to celebrate. He was surprised to find the bottle empty. He had thought that several inches still remained within it. For that matter, he had thought that some food also remained, though the serving board was now empty.

Shrugging, he headed for the stair. He would charm more out of the pantry. He was ravenous after the night's adventures.

XIV.

He had threaded them all through Rondoval; and now, as the day slackened, he was resolved to lie in wait, to learn whether they worked, to see what they snared.

In a small sitting room he had not previously frequented, he seated himself at the center of his web and waited. He had set himself no other chore than thinking during this period, but that was all right. Fine, in fact.

The strands lay all about him, silver-gray, taut. He had strung them throughout Castle Rondoval that afternoon, like a ghostly series of trip-wires. He could feel them all, knew where each one led.

By now, he had come to the conclusion that they were not visible to other people under normal conditions. Summoning them, noting them, using them, were all a part of his power—the same power that had led him to this place he now knew to be his home. The others who had dwelled here had also possessed it, along with other knowledge and aptitudes—things about which he was still learning. He wondered about them . . .

Mor had taken him as a baby, the old man had said, and exchanged him for the real Daniel Chain. If he had been born here and removed at the time of the battle which had so damaged this place, then these depredations had occurred a little over twenty years ago—presuming that time behaved in approximately the same fashion here as it did there. Such being the case, he wondered concerning the cause of the conflict and its principals. All things considered, it would seem that his parents had been the losers and were doubtless now dead.

He wondered about them. There were intact portraits in various rooms, one of which could have been that of the Lord Det, the author of the journals, the man he judged to be his father. The portraits were untitled, though, and he had no idea at all as to his mother's identity.

His wrist tingled slightly, but there were no signs yet from the strands he had laid. He watched the hallway darken beyond the door. He thought of the world in which he now found himself, speculating as to whether he might have been able to see threads in his own, had he known to try. He wondered what it would have been like to have grown up here. Now, now he felt a proprietory attitude toward the place, even if he did not understand its full history, and he resented the presence of the intruder.

For an intruder there was. He knew it as surely as if he had seen him lurking about. Knew it not just from the fact that everything edible and drinkable which he left about had a way of disappearing, but from dozens of small telltales—suddenly bright doorknobs which he knew to have been dusty, minor rearrangements of articles, abrupt scuff marks in unused hallways. It added up to a sense of the presence of another. Irrationally, he felt as if Rondoval itself were passing him warnings.

And he had worked this spell out carefully, partly by intuition, partly from hints in his father's books. It seemed that everything had been done correctly. When the visitor moved, he would know it, he would act—

Again, the tingling. Only this time it did not pass, and his finger jerked toward a single strand. He touched it, felt it pulse. Yes. And this one led to a ruined tower to the rear. Very well. He caught it between his fingers and began the manipulations, the sensations in his wrist increasing as he worked.

Yes. A moving human body, male, had disturbed his alarm. Even now the thread swelled, pulsed with power, was firmly fixed to the intruder.

Pol smiled. The workings of his will flowed forth along the line, freezing the man in his tracks.

". . . And now, my friend," Pol muttered, "it is time for us to meet. Come to me!"

The man began descending the tower stair, his movements slow and mechanical. He tried to resist what he realized to be a spell, but this had no effect upon his progress. Perspiration broke out over his brow and his teeth were clenched. He watched his feet proceed steadily down the stair, then along a hallway. He tried catching at doorframes and pillars as he passed them, but his hands were always torn free. Finally, they vanished beneath his cloak.

Moments later, he held a long climbing cord, which he hurriedly knotted about his right wrist. He attached a small grappling hook to its farther end and cast it up and out through a high window. He tugged several times upon it, saw that it held. Seizing the cord with both hands then, he began to pray to Dwastir, protector of thieves, as he threw his weight upon it.

Pol frowned. He realized that the other's progress had ceased. He increased his efforts, but the intruder was no longer coming toward him. Rising, with a curse, he walked out into the twilit hallway, following the filament, candles flaring as he neared them. It only occurred to him after he had gone some distance that the other might also be some sort of an adept. How else could he have halted in the midst of such a summons as he had received to walk in this direction? Perhaps he should simply call Moonbird, to overwhelm the intruder with sheer force . . .

No. This act of defense, he decided, should be his own, if at all possible. He felt a need to test his powers against another, and the defense of Rondoval seemed as if it should be a personal thing now that he and the place had claims on one another.

He might have missed the small, darkly clad man, had not the angle of the silver-gray strand directed his attention upwards. There, he saw the kicking feet, as if they still strove to walk, as the figure dragged itself upward using armpower alone.

"Amazing," Pol observed, reaching out and touching the strand again. "Halt all your efforts to flee me. Climb back down. Return. Now!"

The man ceased his climbing and his boots grew still. He hung for a moment, began to lower himself. Then, at a point about ten feet overhead, in full if not proper obedience to his order, the man let go the cord at a certain moment of its sway and, heels together, dropped directly toward him.

Pol leaped backward, struck the wall with his shoulder, spun aside. The man struck the floor nearby, fulfilling the order, then began to run.

Recovering, Pol manipulated the strand so that it slipped and caught like a lariat about the other's ankles. The man sprawled.

He moved to the other's side, maintaining the tension upon the filament. The man rolled, a knife appearing in his hand, thrusting toward his thigh. Pol, already alert, danced away, a loop appearing in the strand and twisting itself about the other's wrists, tightening.

The blade fell to the floor and skidded a great distance along it, vanishing from sight in the far shadows. The man's wrists were drawn together as tightly as his ankles. His pale eyes now found Pol's and regarded him without expression.

"I must say you are extremely imaginative in executing an order," Pol remarked. "You take me literally when you choose to and take advantage of every loophole when you do not. You must have some legal background."

The other smiled.

"I have at times been very close to the profession," he said in a soft, almost sweet voice, and then he sighed. "What now?"

Pol shook his head.

"I don't know. I've no idea who you are or what you want. My security as well as my curiosity require that I find out."

"My name is Mouseglove, and I mean you no harm."

"Then why have you been sneaking about here, stealing food?"

"A man must eat—and my own desire for security demanded that I sneak about. All that I know of you is that you are a sorcerer and dragon-rider. I was somewhat reluctant to come up and introduce myself."

"Reasonable enough," Pol observed. "Now, if I knew why you are here at all, I might be in a better position to sympathize with your plight."

"Well, yes," said Mouseglove. "I am, as they say, a thief. I came here for the purpose of stealing a collection of jewelled figurines belonging to the Lord Det. It was a commissioned thing. I simply had to deliver them to a Westerland buyer, collect my fee and go my way. Unfortunately, Det caught me at it—much as you've trammeled me here—and had me confined to one of the cells below. By the time I managed to escape, a war was in progress. The castle was under attack and the beseigers were about to break in. I saw Det destroyed in a magical contest with an old sorcerer, and I decided that the safest place for me was back in my cell. I lost my way below, however, and wound up in a cavern, where I slept. I was awakened to the sight of you flying off on a great dragon. I left there, came up here, was hungry. I couldn't get at the food in the pantry."

"I don't understand why you remained around at all."

Mouseglove licked his lips.

"I had to check," he said finally, "to see whether the figurines were still about."

"Are they?"

"I couldn't locate them. But from the growth of the trees hereabout, I began to realize that more time than I'd thought had passed while I slept . . ."

"About twenty years, I'd guess," Pol said, freeing Mouseglove's legs. "Are you hungry?"

"Yes."

"So am I. Let's go and eat. If I release your hands, will you use them to help me carry food, rather than try to knife me?"

"I'd much rather knife you on a full stomach."

"That'll do."

Pol untwisted the final loop.

"I'd give a lot to know that trick," Mouseglove said, watching him.

"Let's go to the pantry," Pol said, "and on the way, I want you to tell me how my father died."

Mouseglove rose to his feet.

"Your father?"

"The Lord Det."

"There *was* a baby," Mouseglove said.

"Twenty years," Pol replied.

Mouseglove rubbed his brow.

"Twenty . . . That is hard to believe. I don't see how it could happen."

"You were trapped in a grand sleep spell, along with the dragons. I must have released you when I awakened Moonbird. You had to have been asleep nearby."

They began to walk.

"There *were* dreams of dragons, now you mention it."

He turned and regarded Pol.

"I first saw you in your mother's arms. She burned me when I tried to touch you."

"You knew her?"

"The Lady Lydia . . . Yes. Lovely woman. I suppose I'd best start at the beginning . . ."

"Please do."

They obtained food and drink from the pantry and returned to the library, to spend most of the night talking. When they had finished eating, Pol strummed his guitar absently and listened to the other speak, occasionally pausing to sip from his wineglass. At

one point he struck a chord which made Mouseglove's hair rise
and set his teeth on edge.

"*They* killed my parents?" he said softly. "The villagers?"

"I guess there were other people in the army besides villagers,"
Mouseglove replied. "I even saw centaurs among them. But it was
another sorcerer who actually fought Det—Mor, I think he was
called—"

"Mor?"

"I believe so."

"Go on."

"I think your mother was in the southwest tower when it fell.
At least, that was where she was headed when I saw her with you.
You were discovered alone outside the entrance to it. You were
taken to the main hall. The troops wanted to kill you. Mor saved
you, though, by exchanging you for another child from another
place—or rather, he claimed that he could. Did he?"

"Yes. They killed my parents . . ."

"Twenty years. They'll be older now—perhaps even dead. You
could never locate all of them."

"Those who stoned me had the proper mentality—and their
recognition of my dragonmark says something."

"Pol—Lord Pol—I don't know your story—where you've
been, what it was like, what you've been through, how you came
back—but I'm older than you. There are many things of which I
am not sure, but one that I've had more opportunity than most to
learn. Hate will eat you up, will twist you—moreso, perhaps, if
there is no longer, really, a proper object upon which to vent
it—"

Pol began to speak, but Mouseglove raised his hand.

"Please. Let me finish. It's not just a sermon on good behavior.
You're young, and I got the impression on the way up here that
you had just come into your powers. I've a feeling that this may
be a pivotal point in your life. Looking back on my own, I see
that there were a number of such occasions. Everyone seems to
have a few. It looks to me as if you have not yet given thought to
the path you intend to follow. Old Mor seemed, basically, a white

magician. Your father had a reputation as one of the other sort. I know that things are never really black or white, pure and simple, but after a time one can usually judge from a preponderance of evidence in which direction a great power has led a person, if you see what I mean. If you start looking for revenge after all these years, at this time in your life—using your newfound powers to do it—I've a feeling you may in some ways be twisted by the enterprise, so that everything you touch later on will somehow bear its mark. I tell you this not only because I fear turning another Det loose upon the land, but because you are young and because it will probably hurt you, too."

Pol was silent for a time. Then he struck a chord.

"My father had a staff, a wand, a rod," he said. "You mentioned earlier that Mor broke it into three parts. Tell me again what he said he was going to do with it."

Mouseglove sighed.

"He spoke of something called—I believe—the Magical Triangle of Int. He was going to banish each segment to one point of it."

"That's all?"

"That's all."

"Do you know what it means?"

"No. Do you?"

Pol shook his head.

"Never heard of it."

"What do you think of my assessment of your position?"

Pol took a sip of wine.

"I hate them," he said, as he replaced the glass. "Perhaps my father was an evil man—a black magician. I do not know. But I cannot learn of his death by violence and be unmoved. No. I still hate them. They responded like animals in their ignorance. They treated me badly when I meant them no harm. And I recently heard the story of another man, who meant them well and perhaps went about things incorrectly, but who suffered greatly at their hands. It is not so easy to forgive."

"Pol—Lord Pol. They were afraid. You represented something they must have had good cause to fear if its memory lingered this long, this strongly. As for the other man, who knows? Could there have been some similarity?"

Pol nodded.

"Yes. I understand that he tried to force something new upon them—new, yet like something which had been rejected long ago. I suppose you are right. Have you more to tell me?"

"Not really. I would like to hear your story, though. It seems only a few days since I saw you as a babe."

Pol smiled for the first time in a long while. He refilled their glasses.

"Very well. I would like to tell someone . . ."

Daylight was trickling into the room when Pol opened his eyes. He had slept on the sofa. Mouseglove was curled up on the floor.

He rose and soundlessly made his way downstairs, where he washed and changed his garments. He headed for the pantry to load a breakfast tray. Mouseglove was up by the time he returned, grooming himself, eyeing the food.

As they ate, Mouseglove asked him, "What are your plans now?"

"A little vengeance, I think," Pol replied.

"I was afraid of that," said the other.

Pol shrugged.

"It's easy for you to say, 'Forget it.' They didn't try to kill you."

"I spent time in the hands of your father's jailers."

"But you admit to attempted larceny here. I wasn't doing a damned thing to them, except providing a free floor show. There *is* a distinction."

"You've made up your mind. There is nothing more I can say —save that I would like to leave, if it is all right with you."

"Sure. You're not a prisoner any longer. We'll make you up a food parcel."

"Just these extra loaves here, and some of those other leftovers would be sufficient. I like to travel light."

"Take them. Where are you headed?"

"Dibna."

Pol shook his head.

"I don't know it."

"A port city, to the south. Here." He turned and drew an atlas from a shelf. "There it is," he finally said, pointing.

"Fairly far," Pol remarked, nodding. "A lot of dead country between here and there. I'll take you, though, if you're game."

"What do you mean?"

"Dragonback. I'll fly you down."

Mouseglove paled and gnawed his lip. Then he smiled.

"Of course you jest."

"No, I'm serious. I feel indebted for all the information you've given me. I can postpone burning a few fields and barns for a day or so. I'll take you to Dibna if you're willing to ride with me on Moonbird."

Mouseglove began to pace.

"All right," he finally said, turning on his heel and halting. "If you are sure he'll permit the company of a stranger."

"He'll permit it."

They sailed south on the massive back of the coppery dragon, the sun still low to their left, the cool winds of the retreating night making human conversation difficult.

I wish you had brought the musical instrument.

It's a little crowded for it.

That human is somehow familiar. From dreams, I'd say.

He was tangled in your sleep spell, nearby in the cavern. He dreamt of dragons, he tells me.

Strange . . . I almost feel as if I could talk with him.

Why not try?

HELLO, HUMAN!

Mouseglove started, looked down, smiled.

You are Moonbird? he asked.

Yes.

I am Mouseglove. I steal things.

We slept together?

Yes.

I am glad to meet you.

Likewise . . .

The small man relaxed noticeably after that, leaning back at one point to remark to Pol, "This is not at all as I'd thought it would be. He seems awfully familiar. Those dreams . . ."

"Yes."

They watched the countryside dip and rise beneath them, greenwood, brown ridges, blue waters. They passed an occasional isolated dwelling, traced a track that turned into a road. There were several orchards, a farmhouse. To the left, where the land sloped, Pol saw the cluster of stones where he had slept. His mouth tightened.

Follow the road.

Yes.

The village would be coming up soon. Might as well take another look, during daylight hours, he decided. Might even be able to frighten a few people.

Below, he saw a centaur on a hilltop, staring upward. What was it Mouseglove had said? "I even saw centaurs among them?"

Dive. Give him a good look.

They dropped rapidly. The centaur turned and ran. Pol chuckled.

"It's a beginning," he remarked, as they climbed again.

Ahead, Lord. More of the flying things. Let me smash them.

Pol squinted. The dark metallic shapes were circling over a small area. He looked below.

Aren't there more of them on the ground?

Yes. But those in the air will be easier to get at.

He felt Moonbird's body grow warm beneath him.

But isn't there someone—human—down there with them? It looks like a girl.

Yes.

Even from this height, he could see the color of her hair . . .

Let's go after the ones on the ground. Be careful not to harm the girl.

Moonbird sighed and wisps of a grayish gas seemed to curl from his nostrils, to be immediately dispersed by the winds.

Humans always complicate things.

Suddenly, they were diving. The scene below enlarged rapidly. Pol was certain now that it was Nora, at the center of a triangle formed by three of the flying things. These seemed more elaborately constructed than those he had encountered in the night. They had landed and were moving—hopping and crawling—along the ground, closing in on her. She, in turn, was using the rough terrain to keep them at a distance, maneuvering so that rocks and stands of shrubbery barred their ways, as she worked her way toward the fringes of the forest. Once she got in among the trees, he decided, she might well be able to elude them. Still, she might not.

He smelled an odor of rotten eggs now, as the results of some internal chemical reaction of Moonbird's seemed to fill the air about him.

Suddenly, Moonbird's wings were extended and his body was assuming a more upright position as he slowed. Pol braced himself. Mouseglove, seated before him, did the same.

The landing was even worse than he had anticipated—a spine-jolting crash that nearly threw him loose from his position. He squeezed with his legs and his knuckles tightened. It was several seconds before he realized that they had come down directly atop one of the devices.

Then Moonbird belched—a moist, disgusting sound, which was accompanied by an intensification of the odor he had detected during their descent. Immediately thereafter, he appeared to be regurgitating. A great stream of noxious liquid spewed from his mouth to drench the second machine nearby. It fumed for several seconds after it struck, then burst into flame.

Pol sought Nora. She now appeared to be retreating as much from them as from the final machine. Suddenly, however, she recognized him.

"Pol!"

"It's all right!" he called back, just as Moonbird advanced and began striking at the device which was now bounding about as if attempting to take flight.

The first blow damaged its right wing. The second shattered it

completely. By then, however, two more had descended and a third was diving, but pulled up and began to circle.

Moonbird belched again and another began to flame. The final one launched itself toward his face.

Pol crouched low, as did Mouseglove, but not so low that he could not see what followed.

Moonbird opened his mouth and raised his forelimbs. There followed a crunching sound, and then he was tearing the wings off the flier.

. . . *Not at all good to eat.*

He spat. The remains fell before him and began to smolder.

Pol looked up. The one remaining bird was climbing higher and higher.

Chase it?

No. I want to help Nora. Wait.

He climbed down and threaded his way through the wreckage.

"Hi," he said, taking hold of her hand. "What happened? What are they?"

"They're Mark's," she replied. "The same sort of thing that came to save him. He sent them for me . . ."

"Why?"

"He wants me. He said he'd come for me."

"And you don't want to go to him?"

"Not now."

"Then I think we'd better go see him and straighten this out. Where is he?"

She looked at him, at Moonbird, back at him.

"South, I believe," she finally said, "at a forbidden place they sometimes call Anvil Mountain."

"Do you know how to find it?"

"I think so."

"Have you ever ridden a dragon before?"

"No."

He squeezed her hand and turned.

"Come on. It's fun. This one's named Moonbird."

She did not move.

"I'm afraid," she said. "The last dragons anyone saw were Devil Det's . . ."

He nodded.

"This one's okay. But let me ask you whether you're more afraid of this Mark guy and his gadgets or a tame, housebroken pet I just rode in on."

She shook her head.

"Where did you find it? How do you control it? Is it true about your being related to the House of Rondoval? You said you were a traveler—"

"Too much. Too long to tell you now."

". . . Because, if you are of Rondoval—as they said—then that probably *is* one of Det's dragons."

"He's mine now. But I won't lie to you. I didn't before, either. I just didn't know then. —Yes, I'm related to that House. I'd like to help you, though. Will you show me where this guy lives? I want to talk with him."

She studied his face. He met her eyes. Abruptly, she nodded.

"You're right. He means harm. Perhaps we can reason with him. How do we mount?"

"Let me introduce you first . . ."

As the ground dropped away beneath them, Pol leaned past Nora and told Mouseglove, "There's going to be a little detour on the way to Dibna. I want to visit the person who controls these things."

Mouseglove nodded.

"You postponing your revenge, too?" he asked.

Pol reddened.

"Revenge?" Nora inquired. "What does he mean?"

"Later," Pol snapped. "Tell me about forbidden places."

"They are areas containing leftover things from the old days, when people still used that sort of equipment.

"They are supposed to be haunted," she added.

"I've heard similar stories," Mouseglove put in. "Seen some artifacts, too, in my line of work. The day you were taken away, I heard Mor speak of some sort of balance. Our world went the way that it did, the one he was taking you to went the other way. The two ways seem basically incompatible, and attempts to combine them are dangerous. I got the impression Det might have been doing something along those lines."

"So Mark could be a greater menace than is immediately obvious?"

"It seems that way."

Pol shaded his eyes and stared ahead, locating the tiny dot the bird-thing had become.

"We seem to be headed in the same direction."

"What revenge?" Nora said.

"I'm not sure. Let it go, huh?" He glowered at the small thief, who smiled back at him. "An intention is less than a deed," he said, "less even than an attempt." His gaze grew unfocussed. He seemed to pluck at something in the air. "You're a fine one to preach," he added, long moments later, as the smaller man clutched suddenly at his chest, "when you've got my figurines inside your shirt."

Mouseglove blanched, then fell into a spell of coughing.

"I'll deal with you later," Pol said. "I doubt you'll be running off in the meantime. Right now, though, I think I'm beginning to see what Mor meant about a menace when he was bringing me here."

"I can explain—" Mouseglove began.

"Old Mor is the one who brought you to our land?" Nora said.

"Yes."

"That is very interesting. For he is the one I told about Mark when it happened. He seemed ill at the time, though."

Pol nodded.

"He wasn't well."

The character of the land began to shift beneath them. The forest grew thinner. A large river which had followed roughly parallel to their course in the west narrowed, finally passed beneath them and vanished into the southeast. Exposed areas of land were lighter in color now, shading over toward yellow.

The dark speck that was the surveillance flier disappeared from Pol's sight far ahead. It was not until afternoon that they encountered more of them. They first saw several wheeling at a great height far ahead. They dipped lower and moved in their direction, half a dozen of them.

Pol felt a sudden tension in Moonbird's neck and it seemed that the dragon began to grow warmer.

More to smash . . .

Wait, Pol instructed. *They don't seem to be attacking. I think he has sent us an escort.*

Smash escort.

Not so long as they keep their distance.

. . . Some time later.

Wait.

They continued on until the shape of Anvil Mountain appeared low on the horizon in the afternoon light. Their escort had maintained a regular flight about them for hours, unvarying. As they drew nearer, they saw that more of the birds patrolled the skies above the flat-topped height. Below, the land had assumed a bleaker aspect—yellow, streaked with red, dotted with gray and russet outcrops of stone; jagged cracks ran in dry, unpatterned profusion, as on a dropped, earthenware pot; small, scrubby bushes, wind-twisted, clung to the slopes of hills.

The mountain stood larger now, and they could make out a skyline atop it—white, green, gray and reflecting backdrop to many movements. Pol looked about as they drew closer and he felt Moonbird stiffen, then change his course slightly to conform with the movements of the dark fliers.

Go where they take us, for they are surely taking us to him, he ordered.

Moonbird did not reply, but altered course several times as they neared the city on the rock, rising and swinging to the west, beginning a gradual approach to the great flat-roofed building near the center of the complex. Peering downward, Pol saw a tall, red-haired man standing upon a terrace outside what appeared to be a penthouse dwelling. A flying machine of unusual design rested upon a gridded landing area behind the structure. A number of man-sized machines of unknown function moved about in the vicinity.

"More magic," Mouseglove muttered.

"No," said Pol. "Not at all."

He felt Nora's hand upon his arm then, gripping it.

"You know this guy pretty well, don't you?" he asked her.

"Know him? I've been in love with him for years," she replied. "But I'm afraid of him, too, now. He's changed a lot."

"Well, we seem to have a landing clearance. Let's go and talk with him. If you want him to stop bothering you, tell him so and I'll back you up. If you don't, now's your chance to straighten things out."

Down, Moonbird. Land in the clear area.

They descended into a much smoother landing than the previous one. His ears rang faintly as the winds finally ceased whistling about them. He climbed down and assisted Nora to descend. He heard her gasp.

"His eye! It *was* injured!"

Pol turned. The man in the khaki jumpsuit with numerous bulging pockets was now approaching, a peculiar device which covered his left eye changing color as he left the shade, becoming a bright, then deep blue. A vivid scar passed down his forehead above it, emerged on his cheek below it. Pol stepped forward to meet him.

"I'm Pol Detson," he said. "Nora wants to talk to you. So do I."

Mark halted at a distance of about two meters and studied him. Finally, he nodded curtly.

"I'm Mark Marakson." He immediately turned to look at Moonbird. "I've never seen a dragon before . . . Gods, he's big!"

He returned his attention to Pol, not even glancing at Nora.

"Detson . . . Magician?"

"I suppose so."

"I don't understand magic."

"I'm still working at it myself."

Mark gestured suddenly, a sweeping motion of his left arm, apparently intended to take in the entire city.

"This I understand," he said.

"Me, too. There's a lot of it where I come from."

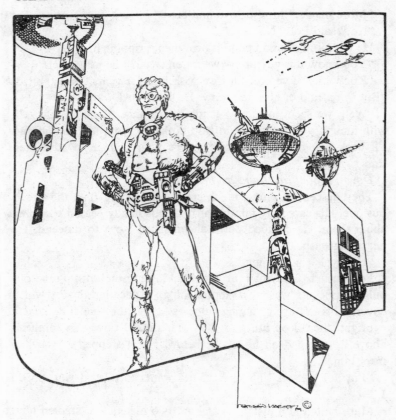

Mark rubbed the scar on his cheek.

"What do you mean? Where is that?" he asked.

"We are step-brothers," Pol replied. "Your parents raised me, in a land much like this place you have restored. Excuse me if I stare, but you do bear Dad a very strong resemblance."

Mark turned away, paced several steps, returned.

"You're joking," he said at last.

"No. Really. For most of my life, I bore the name you were given as a child."

"Which is?"

"Dan Chain."

"Dan Chain," Mark repeated. "I rather like that . . . but how could this be? I did learn only recently that I'd been adopted, but this— Too much coincidence! I can't believe it."

"Well, it's true, and it's not entirely coincidence. In fact— Wait a minute . . ."

Pol dug in his hip pocket, withdrew his wallet. He opened it and flipped through the card case.

"Here," he said, stepping forward, extending it. "These are pictures of Mother and Dad."

Mark reached toward him, accepted the wallet, stared.

"These aren't drawn!" he said. "There's a very sophisticated technology involved!"

"Photography's been around for awhile," Pol replied.

The lens brightened as Mark stared.

"Their names?" he asked.

"Michael Chain—and Gloria."

"I— Yes, I see myself in these faces. May I— Have you others?"

"Yes. I have some more further down. You can take those. Just slide them out. Yes, like that."

Mark passed the wallet back.

"What sort of work does he do?"

This time Pol made a sweeping gesture.

"He builds things. Designs them, rather. Much on the order of what you've apparently been doing here."

"I would like to meet him."

"I believe he'd like you. But I was thinking—as I acquired certain recent skills of my own—on the means by which I was brought to this world. It would take more research and some experimenting, but I believe I could learn to duplicate Mor's stunt in transporting me. It's occurred to me that a guy like you might not be happy here—especially after the story I heard—and I wondered whether you might be interested in going to the place from which I came. You might like it a lot better there."

Mark finally looked up from the photos and inserted them into a small thigh pocket. He stared at Nora as if seeing her for the first time.

"She told you what they did to me, to my—stepfather?"

Pol nodded.

"You have my sympathy. I received very similar treatment myself, for different reasons."

"Then you must understand how I feel." He looked again at Moonbird. "Do you have plans for them?"

"At first, I did. But now, no. I can almost understand, almost forgive. That's close enough. The longer I let it go, the less it should bother me. Let them go their ways, I'll go mine."

Mark struck his right fist against his left palm and turned away.

"It is not that easy," he said, pacing again. "For you—a stranger—perhaps. But I lived there, grew up there, knew everyone. I took them a gift. It was rejected under the worst circumstances. Now— Now I'm going to force it upon them."

"You will cause a lot of pain. Not just for them. For yourself, too."

"So be it," Mark said. "They've made their own terms."

"I think I could send you home—a place you'd probably like— instead."

For a moment, Mark looked at him almost wistfully. Then, "No. Maybe afterwards," he said. "Now it's no longer the gift, but its acceptance. In a matter of weeks, I'll be ready to move. Later . . . We'll see."

"You ought to take some time to think it over."

"I've had more than enough time. I've done plenty of thinking while recovering from our last encounter."

"If I could send you back for just a little while—and you rethought it in a different place—you might get a whole new perspective, decide that it isn't really worth doing . . ."

Mark took a step nearer, lowered his head. His new eye hummed and the lens shone gold.

"You seem awfully eager to be rid of me," he said slowly. Then he turned and looked again at Nora. "Might she be the reason?"

"No," Pol said. "She's known you for years, me for only a few days. There is nothing between us."

"A situation you would probably like to remedy in my absence."

"That's your idea, not mine. I'd like to keep you from making a mistake I almost made. But she can talk for herself."

Mark turned toward her.

"Do you want to get rid of me, also?" he asked.

"Stay," she told him. "But leave the village alone. Please."

"After what they did?"

"They showed you their feelings. They were too harsh, but you'd scared them."

"You're on their side!"

"I was the one who warned you."

". . . And his side!" He gestured at Pol, lens flashing. "Magic! Dragons! He represents everything archaic and reactionary! He stands in the way of progress! And you prefer him to me!"

"I never said that!"

She took a step forward, beginning to reach toward him. He turned away. He waved his right fist in Pol's face.

"I could kill you with one hand. I was a blacksmith."

"Don't try it," Pol said. "I was a boxer."

Mark looked up. Moonbird looked down at him.

"You think that ancient beast makes you invincible? I, too, have servants."

He raised his left hand, peeled back the sleeve. A large control bracelet, covering half his forearm, gleamed in the space between them. His fingers danced upon the studs. The man-sized machines all turned in their direction and began to advance.

Pol raised his right hand. His loose sleeve fell back. The dragonmark moved visibly upon his pulse.

"It is not too late," Pol said, "to stop what I think I see coming."

"It is too late," Mark replied.

One by one, the machines faltered and grew still, some emitting static and strange noises, others ceasing all movement abruptly, without sound. Mark ran his fingers over his controls once again, but nothing responded.

"Dad used to call that my poltergeist effect," Pol stated. "Now—"

Mark swung at him. Pol ducked and drove a fist into his mid-section. Mark grunted and bent slightly. Pol caught him on the jaw with a left jab. He'd a chance for a second blow to the other's face but pulled the punch for fear of striking the eye prosthesis. In that off-balance moment of hesitation, Mark swung his entire left arm like a club, his heavy bracelet striking Pol on the side of the head.

Pol fell to his knees, covering his head with both arms. He saw a boot coming and fell to the side to avoid it.

Squash? Burn?

He realized he had come into contact with the great beast.

No, Moonbird! No!

But a low rumble from the dragon caused Mark to draw back, looking upward, raising his hands.

Vision dancing, Pol saw the strands all about them. That red one . . .

From the corner of his normal eye, Mark saw the fallen man gesture with his left hand. He moved to kick at him again and felt his legs grow immobile. He began to topple.

He struck and lay there, paralyzed from the waist down. As he struggled to prop himself with his arms, he saw that the other had risen to his knees again and was still rubbing his head. Suddenly, there was an arm about his shoulder. He looked up.

"Nora . . ."

"Please, Mark. Say you won't hurt our village, or any of the others."

He tried to pull away from her.

"You never cared for me," he said.

"That's not true."

"The first good-looking stranger comes along, you lay your claim and send him to get rid of me . . ."

"Don't talk like that."

He turned into a sitting position.

"Flee while you have the chance," he said. "Warn the villages or not, as you choose. It will make no difference. I will be coming. I will take what I want. That includes you. What I bring with

me will be more than sufficient to deal with a dragon—or a whole family of them. Go! Tell them I hate them all. Tell them—"

"Come on, Nora," Pol said, rising. "There is no reasoning with the man."

He held out his hand. She rose and took it.

"I suppose I would be wise," he said to Mark, "to kill you. But she would never forgive me. And you are the son of the only parents I knew. So you have some time. Use it to reconsider your plan. If you come, as you said you would, I will be waiting. I've no desire to be the villagers' champion. But there is a balance you would upset which could bring great danger to us all."

As he helped Nora to mount Moonbird, he saw that Mouseglove had vanished. He looked about the rooftop, but the man was nowhere in sight.

He climbed up behind her. He looked down at Mark.

"Don't come," he said.

"I feel your magic," Mark said softly. "I will find a way to stop it. It must be a wave phenomenon, tuned by your nervous system—"

"Don't lose any sleep over it."

Moonbird, home!

He felt the great muscles bunch beneath him. Moonbird was running, hopping, gliding. They sailed out over the edge of the roof and began to climb.

"He will not be paralyzed for good, will he?"

Pol shook his head.

"An hour or so. The strands are tangled, not knotted."

"Strands? What do you mean?"

"He's a prisoner inside himself. His body will recover soon."

"He will destroy us," she said.

"He's got quite an impressive base," said Pol, looking down. "You may be right. I hope not."

The sun had begun its long slide westward. Once more, the winds sang about them. Below and behind, Mark's mechanical servants began to move long before he did. He had not really paid attention to the third person to regard him from the back of Moonbird. Now, the shadowy image of the small man was submerged by the torrent of his hate for the other, passing altogether into oblivion.

Clouds passed. His lens darkened. The bracelet began to function once again.

XV.

The prototype blue-bellied, gray-backed tracer-bird with the wide-angle eye and the parabola ear followed the dragon-riders north. A series of the larger fliers followed it at well-spaced intervals, to serve as relay points for the spy broadcasts. So far, however, the tracer-bird had not yet gained sufficiently upon its objective that it had anything to transmit. Had it been nearer, it would have overheard portions of the story Pol had recently recounted to Mouseglove. But as it was not, it did not even hear Nora's questions.

"I am surprised that you realized this much of your heritage so quickly, so fully. But even so, Mark has had time to build his strength and you have not. How would you oppose a large flight of those birds, and a mass of the ground machines? And I thought that I saw men back there, too. Or dwarves . . . Supposing he has a large army? Have you any plan at all?"

Pol was silent for a time, then, "There was an instrument of power which had belonged to my father," he said. "With it, I think I might be able to command all of the, uh, resources of Rondoval. If I could get hold of it before Mark begins to move, I would have something formidable to throw against him. I'm still hazy on the geography and the political setup of this land, though. I don't know how much territory and how many population centers he would be moving against, or what the local defense apparatus is. All of the books I have are older than I am . . . I have maps, too, but I'm not sure what goes where."

"I can show you," she said, "and tell you about it, when we get to the maps."

"But I'll be dropping you in your village."

"No! You can't do that! I'm afraid. He might come for me again. Who would stop him this time?"

"You might not like Rondoval."

"It's got to be better than Anvil Mountain. You don't know any magic that could change him back, do you? To the way he was a few years ago?"

"I don't think any magic can undo what life has done to a person, or a person to himself. I'm sorry."

"I thought you'd say that. The wise folk all seem to talk the same way."

She began to cry softly, for the first time that day. Though it was gaining, the tracer-bird did not hear this either. Pol did, but he was not certain what to say. So he stared ahead and said nothing.

It was dark when they passed above Nora's village and by then Pol had placed his cloak about her shoulders. The stars had come forth in profusion and shone with great brilliance. Pol realized for the first time that he did not recognize any constellations. Moonbird, looking down rather than up, noted the locations of all visible cattle against his return for a late night snack.

* * *

He awoke in a dirty room far below ground level. It seemed to be one of the original ancient chambers in the rock, which the new occupants had not yet gotten around to refurbishing. Possibly it had been some sort of storeroom. It was full of junk, dust and stale air. This was why he had chosen it. It was far from the throbbing, or even the humming of the great machines, and none of the lesser ones had rattled by. As for the small, long-armed, slope-shouldered men with the low brows—they seemed to avoid this quarter.

He ate some of the food he had brought with him. He secreted the parcel of figurines beneath a trash heap.

. . . Had to leave at this stop, he reflected. Once the kid caught on, it was all over. Damned scary, the way he'd plucked the information out of the air. Good thing there was a distraction . . .

. . . How many days' walk to Dibna? Could take the better part of a week, he guessed. Therefore, he needed a good supply of food before he set out . . .

. . . What time was it? Probably the middle of the night, judging by his internal clock. With any luck at all, he'd have

the supplies by morning and be ready to move the following
night . . .

He opened the door slightly and stared out upon the dim corridor. Empty. He was out, along it and up a ramp in a matter of
seconds. The air grew somewhat fresher as he advanced, but was
still warm. Keeping to the darkest ways available, he mounted
until he was several stories above the ground. He heard the distant noises of the factories now, the nearer ones of servant machines passing on mysterious errands.

He stepped out beneath stars. There was that low structure he had not investigated earlier, some illumination within it now. Off to the left and standing higher was the building from which he had descended that afternoon. Yes. There was the bridge above the avenue by which he had crossed over . . .

He had seen Pol and Nora fly off, heading back to the north. Good that they had gotten free. He wished them no ill, particularly at the hands of that tall, red-haired man with the glowing eye. He had a fear of something even worse than magic should he fall that one's prisoner, and he resolved to avoid him at all costs.

They may keep the food someplace around here . . .

He was attracted again by the small, dimly lighted structure. It was probably not a supply house, but it might be prudent to know what it was—situated in such a prominent position—in case any threats resided there.

He moved nearer, circling to place a blank wall between his advance and whoever was inside. His tread was soundless. He was alert for trip-wires, sentries.

Finally, he touched the gray wall, slid his hand along it, flattened himself and waited a moment. Then he edged his way to the corner, peered around it, passed beyond it, moved toward the window near the door.

Nothing. The view was blocked by some sort of equipment. He dropped and passed beneath it, hastily passed the door. He tried the next window.

Yes. There were two men, off toward the right, rear, seated before what appeared to be a group of glowing windows which he knew did not penetrate the wall. But the angle was too sharp here, and the window through which he peered was closed.

He passed on, turned the next corner, advanced even more cautiously toward an opened window. Reaching it, he dropped to one knee and looked in toward the right.

He heard an occasional voice, though it took him several moments to realize that the figures within were not speaking. The words seemed to emerge from the wall before them. He squinted, he concentrated, he breathed a few words to Dwastir.

Suddenly, he recognized one of the scenes on the wall. The peripheral screens held strangely accented aerial views of country-scape, not unlike some over which he had passed earlier on dragonback. But the central one, toward which the two men were leaning, showed, in much sharper detail, the library at Rondoval, where he had spent so many hours. It was as if he were peering in through the end windows. There was Pol at the desk, candles flickering near at hand, a number of books opened before him. Nora was dozing on the couch.

Abruptly, he realized that the larger of the two men viewing the screen was Mark Marakson. He fought an impulse to flee. Both men seemed too involved with the display to be exceptionally wary. So, checking about him periodically, Mouseglove continued to stare. The men's attitudes, the surreptitious quality of the enterprise, both convinced him he must be witnessing something important.

Time slipped by, with Pol occasionally muttering something about the points of a triangle. Once or twice, this drew a sleepy reply from Nora.

An hour, perhaps longer, passed before Pol spoke again. He was smiling as he looked up.

"A pyramid, a great labyrinth and the Itzan well," he said, "in that order. That's the Triangle of Int. Nora?"

"Mm?"

"Can you find them for me in the big atlas?"

"Bring it here." She raised herself upright and rubbed her eyes. "I've never been anyplace far, but I always liked geography. What were they, again?"

Pol was rising, a book in his hands, when the view was suddenly blocked by a movement of Mark's.

Mark half-rose to scrawl something on a writing sheet, which he folded and inserted into one of his pockets. Pol's and Nora's voices had resumed, partly muffled now. Mark leaned forward, moving his face close to the screen.

"I've got you," he said softly. "Whatever the weapon you seek to use against me, you shall not have it. Not when I have three chances—"

His voice broke. He raised a hand as if to cover his eyes, forgetting for a moment the red lens that he wore.

"Damn!"

He turned away and Mouseglove ducked quickly, but not before he had glimpsed the screen and what might have been an embrace.

* * *

Moonbird drowsed, riding a thermal to a great height, then dropping into a long glide. When he lowered the night-membrane over his eyes, he saw another thermal, like a wavering red tower, ahead and to his left. Unconsciously, he shrugged himself in that direction. He'd a full belly now, and it was pleasant just to drift home, watching the dreams form in the other chamber of his mind.

He saw himself bearing the young master and the lady across a great desert, heading toward a mountain that was not a mountain. Yes, he had passed that way once before, long ago. He remembered it as very dry. He saw a gleaming bird pass and lay an egg which bloomed into a terrible flower. This, he felt, he should remember.

He glided into the next thermal and rose again. It was good to be out of the cavern once more. And he saw that they would be leaving for the dry place tomorrow. That was good, too. Perhaps he would sleep in the courtyard, where he could show them the carrier and the saddle come morning. They would be up early, and they would be needing them . . .

Near to the tower's top, he spread his wings and commenced a long glide. Somewhere in his dreams, the one with the strange eye moved, but he was difficult to follow.

* * *

The sun was already high when Pol finished packing the gear. Again, Nora's argument that she would be in greater danger alone

than with him prevailed. He packed two light blades, along with
the food, extra clothing, blankets . . . No armor. He did not want
to push Moonbird to the limits of endurance, or even to slow him
with more than the barest of essentials. Besides, he had learned to
fence in a different school.

How did he know? he wondered, hauling the parcels out to the
carrier the great beast had located for him.

Crossing the courtyard, he placed his hands upon Moonbird's
neck.

How do you know what is needed?

I—Know. Now. Up high. Look!

The massive head turned. Pol followed the direction of its gaze.

He saw the small, blue-bellied, gray-backed thing upon the sill
overhead. It was turned as if watching them. A portion of its
front end caught the sunlight and cast it down toward them.

What is it?

Something I do not know. See how it watches?

*It must be something of his. I wonder how much of my plans it
has learned?*

Shall I upchuck firestuff upon it?

No. Pretend that it is not there. Do not look at it.

He turned and crossed to the castle, entering there. He had
come upon a description of an effect in one of his father's volumes and had been meaning to try it when he had the time.

He hurried up the stair, to halt outside the library where Nora
sat sketching some final maps. Peering in, he saw that she wore
a pale tunic, short gray breeches, a metal belt and sturdy boots
she had located in one of the upstairs wardrobes. Her hair was
bound back by a black strap.

She looked up as Pol entered.

"I am not entirely finished," she said. "There's another page."

"Go ahead."

She completed a drawing she had been making, took up another writing sheet, turned a page, began another map. She
glanced up at Pol and smiled. He nodded.

"Soon," she said.

She worked for several minutes. Finally, she sighed, closed the book and took up the papers.

"Would you step outside for just a moment, please?"

"Your voice sounds strange."

"Yes. I talked too much. Please."

She crossed to the door. He waited beside it. His face was expressionless. She paused.

"Is something wrong?" she asked.

"No. Go out."

His lips, now that she looked closely, did not seem to move in proper time with his words. She passed through the doorway and halted. In the corridor, Pol stood off to the right, fingers to his lips.

"How—?"

"This way," he whispered, taking her hand.

She followed him.

"It is a simulacrum spun of magical strands, my likeness laid upon it. I don't know how long it will last. Maybe all day, maybe only a little while." He began gesturing, slowly at first, then more rapidly. Something took shape between his hands, a faint glow to it. "This one is yours," he said. "It will go back in there and keep mine company, to distract the spy device, while we depart. He's been watching us. I want as good a lead as possible."

Later, Nora seemed to stroll back into the room, taking the hand of Pol, who still stood beside the door. They crossed slowly to a pair of chairs and sat facing one another.

"Lovely weather."

"Yes."

Periodically, one of them would rise and walk about the room. There were a number of things they would do, together and apart, taking perhaps an hour before the sequence began again.

The prototype blue-bellied, gray-backed tracer-bird followed their every step, hung upon their words. It did not turn away at the noises below, or as Moonbird rose above the flagstones, drifted over the far wall, pivoted on the point of a breeze, bore east and vanished.

*   *   *

As the night progressed, Mouseglove had slowly come to feel as if he were a prisoner. Despite several near-disasters, he had remained undetected, gradually enlarging his mental map of the area and developing an awareness of the city's peculiar defenses. But he could find no way off of Anvil Mountain. The perimeters of the plateau were extremely well-patrolled, both by the small men and the half-mechanical caterpillars, as well as being subject to the scrutiny of fixed mechanical eyes and those of the circling birds. It seemed that not even an insect could pass undetected.

Picking lock after lock, he had finally located stores of foodstuffs and transferred what he judged a sufficient quantity to his hiding place. He memorized every niche, every unfrequented passage he came upon. With a thief's eye, he studied the various fixed detection devices from a distance and finally close up, coming to appreciate their functions and some of their weaknesses.

It was only by chance—chance, and Mark's immediate decision to bolster his combat forces above the level he had formerly felt adequate—that Mouseglove happened upon a newly formed ground school for the preliminary training of pilots for a series of manned fliers on which production had been stepped up.

Lying flat on the roof, blocked from overhead detection by an angled air duct, he could hear the words and view the training machine through a grating he had exposed by removing a small panel.

He listened to the entire lecture. When it was over, he had convinced himself. If he could audit just a few more sessions, he would be willing to steal a flier by night and take his chances in the air. Short of finding a hidden tunnel through the rock itself, it seemed the only way to manage an escape.

Feeling a grudging respect for the red-haired man who had brought this city back to life, he returned to his quarters to rest until evening, when he intended spying upon the surveillance center once again and later breaking into the classroom to study the trainer's controls at closer range.

Following a full meal, he slept deeply; one hand upon his dagger, a stolen grenade he knew was some sort of weapon beneath the other.

* * *

Statue-like, an old female and two young stallions stood on a crag in the midst of a stand of dwarf pines, regarding Castle Rondoval.

"There is nothing out of the ordinary," she said.

"I saw lights last night, Stel, and I heard noises. Bitalph, in the south, did report a dragon."

"The place is probably haunted," she said. "Enough has gone on there."

"And what of the dragon?" asked the younger stallion.

"If one has come awake, it will be dealt with—eventually—by those it most oppresses. It could also be a foreign beast."

"Then we should do nothing?"

"Let us watch here, a day and a night. We can take turns. I've no desire to enter the place."

"Nor I."

It was much later in the day that they saw the dragon rise and drift eastward.

"There!"

"Yes."

"What do we do now?"

"Alert the others. It may never return. But then, again, it may."

"It appeared that there were two riders."

"I know."

"You were there on the day of the battle, Stel. Was that one of the old dragons of Rondoval?"

"All dragons look alike to me. But the riders . . . One of them looked like Devil Det himself, younger and stronger than I ever saw him."

"Woe!"

"Alas!"

"Go and spread the word among the folk. And we had best talk with the men of the villages, and with old Mor."

"Mor is gone. A Wise One—Grane—said that he walked the golden road and will not return."

"Then things are becoming difficult. Go! I will investigate further."

"You would enter the castle yourself?"

"Go! Do as I say! Now!"

The youths obeyed her. They knew the look in her eye, and they still feared her hoofs.

* * *

During his evening explorations, Mouseglove was attracted by a series of screams emerging from a small, barred window. Approaching, he ventured one quick glance through the opening, then ducked into a pool of shadow to digest what he had seen and, if possible, to eavesdrop.

The first impression had shaken him. But upon reflection, he wondered whether the small man in the reclining chair had indeed been covered with snakes. The black things did seem overlong to qualify for serpenthood, and their farther ends did all appear to be attached to the large metal box nearby. Also, their movements could have been a result of the man's own thrashings. Mark had stood nearby with a small metal case in his hand, turning something on the face of the unit.

He listened to the shrieks a little longer, wondering for what offense the man might be undergoing discipline. Wondering, too, whether anything was to be gained by remaining, or by venturing another look.

There was silence. He waited, but the cries did not resume. He decided to remain. There came faint sounds of movement from within.

Finally, he could bear it no longer. He rose for another glimpse.

Mark, facing away from the window, was detaching what now appeared to be a series of shiny black ropes from the supine form, coiling them and placing them in compartments within the large box. The smaller man's eyes were open, staring up at the ceiling. When the last of the leads were removed, he stirred weakly. Mark passed him a glass of something pink and he drank from it.

"How do you feel?" the large man asked.

"Shaky," the other replied, flexing his arms, his legs. "But everything's all right again."

"Did it hurt?"

"No. Not really."

"You screamed a lot."

"I know. Some were blue, but most were red."

"The screams?"

"Yes. And I could smell them."

"Excellent. You were a brave man to volunteer for this, and I want to thank you."

"I was happy to serve."

"Tell me more about it."

"I tasted the colors, too—and the sounds."

"It was a fine mix, then. Pity it only has such a short range. There are all sorts of problems in scaling it up, too . . . I wish I had more time."

"What do you call the—thing that did it?"

Mark hefted the small unit.

"For want of a better name, I call it a jumble box. It smears your sensory inputs, mixes them. Instant synesthesia."

The man gestured toward the huge unit to his right.

"That didn't do it? Just the little one you're holding?"

"That's right. The other just recorded what was happening. If you didn't hurt, tell me why you cried out so much?"

"I— I couldn't understand what was happening. Everything was still there, but it was changed . . . It scared me."

"No pain?"

"No one place that hurt. Just a—feeling that disaster was coming. Most of the time, it kept getting worse. Sometimes, though—"

"What?"

"There were moments of great pleasure."

"You were able to count all right."

"Yes . . . Most of the numbers were yellow. Some tasted sour."

"Did you feel you could have gotten up, walked about?"

"Maybe. If I'd have thought of it. It was hard to think. Too much was wrong."

"You are a brave man, and I thank you again. I will not forget this service. Now, let's test your reflexes."

Mouseglove heard some instruments being shifted about. Silently, he slid off through the night.

* * *

It was difficult for Stel to place her hoofs quietly on stone and tile unless she moved very slowly. This she did, however, with the patience of a huntress and former commando.

Memories returned to her as she passed through the great hall where she had stood dripping blood and sweat that final day of the battle. Ah! the stallions had had much work that night . . . She recalled the sorcerers' confrontation, and her eyes automatically sought that ruined area of ceiling which had settled Det for good, before he could call upon his hidden powers. Much of the rubble beneath had been cleared for the removal of his body. She recalled how Mor had borne it away into the west . . .

She paused periodically and stood listening. Her ears pricked forward. There were voices. Somewhere up higher, to the left.

She crossed the gallery, came to the foot of the stair, halted again. Yes, up there . . .

Slowly, keeping near to the wall, she began to climb. The place appeared to be in better condition than she had remembered.

As she made her way along the hall, the voices came louder. To her right now, that third door . . .

She noted that the door was ajar. Approaching, she stopped directly beside it. She heard nothing from within, not even the sounds of breathing. Venturing farther forward, she looked around the corner, then drew back in puzzlement.

The couple had just seated themselves, facing one another—the young man with the white streak through his hair and the slim blonde girl. But . . . These were the same people she had seen departing on dragonback. She had not seen them return. Strange . . .

She looked again.

More than strange . . .

The girl's face seemed to be melting, pieces of it falling, drifting away, decomposing in the air. The man—who still bore a striking resemblance to old Det—seemed totally oblivious to the fact that portions of his left arm and right thigh appeared to be unravelling, as though he were composed of thin strips of cloth wound about nothing.

Fascinated, Stel did not retreat, but stared in frank astonishment as the couple came apart. Finally, she moved forward and entered the room. What was left of the pair paid her no heed whatsoever.

"Lovely weather."

"Yes . . ."

The man's face now began to melt, the girl's garments ran from her body like liquid, drifted in the air currents like strands of silk. Their conversation continued.

". . . Though it could rain."

"That is true."

The man rose to his foot and crossed to the girl.

"You have lovely eyes."

She rose slowly.

Stel watched them embrace, losing larger and larger pieces of themselves every moment, to drift tinsel-like before her, fading from view as they crossed the room.

"I-arrooowarnn . . ."

The words slowed and deepened, the mouths were gone, the hair went up like smoke. Another half-minute, and they had intertwined and vanished. Stel whinnied and backed away. She had never before seen the like of it. Superstitious dreads rose to harry her.

The prototype blue-bellied, gray-backed tracer-bird now focussed its attention upon her as she circled the room, studying it carefully without paying real attention to the opened atlas, as she retreated out the door and into the corridor beyond, her hoofs clattering rapidly as she passed down the corridor.

*   *   *

Mouseglove heard the great doors opening below and made it to an appropriate vantage in time to see the metal birdforms launched like blown leaves into the dark sky, where they rose to swirl beneath stars, then assumed a formation which tightened itself as it wound and unwound, took its course and passed in a direction he deemed to be roughly southeast. This troubled him as he made his way to the surveillance center. He managed the approach once more and heard Mark within, cursing and giving orders. The one glimpse he got of the screens showed nothing of interest.

He did not understand Mark's, "They're gone! More of that magic, I suppose. That damned centaur had something to do with it! Bring me a centaur!"

Mouseglove decided to leave it at that. Less now than at any other time, did he desire to fall into the hands of the ruddy giant the small men treated like a god. As he backed away, though, the words, ". . . At the triangle's point!" reached him from within. It would not be until later, however, that these would set off lengthy trains of speculation.

Instead, immediate considerations occupied him for the better part of several hours: Time to get out. Things are getting more frantic and life grows less certain. The longer I stay, the worse my chances . . .

The lock on the training room door barely halted his stride. Slowly and carefully, his fingertips found the controls in the model cockpit. He was afraid to make a light.

. . . Funny if I can only fly it with my eyes closed, he reflected. It's scary up there, but it's worse down here. Anyway, better this than a dragon. What did he say about this little lever? Oh, yes . . .

Batteries fully charged, the dark birds fled across the night, the land, the water.

XVI.

East and south. They traveled until fatigue overcame them. Night was rising when they located the island they had marked, and there they slept unmolested. The following day, before the night was fully departed, they crossed over the waters to the land, to sweep above mountains, dwindling rivers, desert. The next night was spent among chilly hills, where Pol reviewed all that he knew concerning their route and destination. The geography here was not congruent with that of his previous world. In that place, the larger land mass he had departed did not even exist, and that over which he was crossing, while similar in places, was not a true match. Distances varied radically between locales which seemed to possess some reconcilability on maps of the two worlds. But they both had pyramids in several places, though the one he sought had the way to its entrance flanked by rows of columns alternating with sphinxes, many of them fallen, damaged, but most still visible. Something in the description he had read seemed to indicate that he should commence his entrance at the end of that way.

* * *

The dark birdforms dotted the mountaintops like statues of prehistoric beasts, wings outspread. Had there been an eye to observe them, it might not even have noted their minute, tropism-like pursuit of the sun across the sky as they recharged their batteries for the night's flight.

The day had beaten its way well on toward evening before they stirred, almost simultaneously, as if shaken by a sudden breeze. They began to flex their wings.

Soon, one by one, they dropped from the heights, caught the air, rose, found their way, found their patterns, resumed their journey . . .

* * *

Pol's wrist began to itch some time before their goal came into view. He felt that it was not just the now-darkening sunburn, and increased his surveillance of the bright and wavering horizon. Minutes later, a pointed dot resolved itself before him and he licked his dry lips and smiled.

Your internal compass seems to be working fine.

I do not know what you mean.

That seems to be it up ahead.

Of course.

"Nora!" His voice came out as a croak. "I see it!"

"I think I do, too!"

It grew before them until there could be no doubt as to its nature. There were no signs of movement anywhere about the dark stone structure. The plain before it was dotted with columns and statues.

Moonbird took them down near the far end of the approach, and Pol's joints creaked as he alighted.

"I can't persuade you to wait here?" he said, as he helped Nora down.

She shook her head.

"If anything happened to you, I'd be in to investigate later, anyway. Waiting would just defer things."

He turned to Moonbird.

Wish I could take you with—but the entrance is too small.

I will guard. You will play sweet music for me later.

I appreciate your confidence.

Pol turned and looked up the sand-scoured roadway, pylons and beasts converging upon the dark rectangle of the structure's entranceway.

. . . Walking into a vanishing point, he mused.

"Okay, Nora. Let's go," he said.

His vision blurred and cleared again as they advanced. For a moment, he thought it was an effect of the brilliant sunlight or the sudden activity after hours of sitting crouched. Then he saw what he took to be flames pouring forth from the opening before them. He flinched.

Nora took hold of his arm.

"What is it?"

"I— Oh, now I see. Nothing."

The flames resolved themselves into great billows of what he had come to think of as the weft of the world. He had never seen them bunched so thickly before, save in the great ball in the caverns of Rondoval—and here they were flapping and drifting freely.

"You must have seen something," she said as they continued on.

"Just an indication of sorts, showing a concentration of magical power."

"What does it mean?"

"I don't know."

She loosened her blade in its scabbard. He did the same.

His right wrist, which had not stopped its itching and tingling, was now throbbing steadily, as if that special part of him which was best suited to deal with such matters was now fully alert.

He brushed his fingertips across the massed strands and felt a surge of power. He tried to locate some clue as to its nature, but nothing suggested itself.

The rod, the rod . . . he concentrated. Somewhere among you . . .

A pale green strand, like milky jade, drifted toward him, separating itself from the mass. As he raised his hand, it seemed drawn toward his fingertips. Once he touched it, he willed it to adhere and held it, knowing that this was the one.

"Now," he told Nora, advancing to the threshold, "I know the way—though I know nothing of what it will be like."

He entered the narrow passage and halted again. The dimness about them deepened to an inky blackness only a few paces ahead.

"Wait," he said, commencing the mental movements which had summoned the phantom dragon from his wrist the night he had fled her village.

It rose and drifted before him again, exactly as it had on that earlier occasion.

Is this a phenomenon I am destined never to use in the absence of danger? he wondered.

Behind him, Nora drew her blade. His chuckle rang hollowly.

"That is my doing," he told her. "It is our light. Nothing more."

"I believe you," she said, "but it seems a good time to have a weapon."

"I can't argue," he replied, beginning to move once again, following the pale thread through the new light.

They came to a flight of steps where they descended perhaps ten meters, the air growing pleasantly cool, then clammy about them. From the foot of the steps, passages ran to the right, the left and straight ahead. The thread followed the one before them. Pol followed the thread.

After several paces, the passage began to slant downward, its angle of steepness seeming to increase as they continued. The air was thick now, and stale, with a scent of old incense or spices buried within its dampness.

The light danced before him. The walls vanished. At first, he thought that they had come to another set of side passages. As he willed his light to brighten and move, however, he saw that they had come into a room.

He sent the dragon-light darting before him, outlining the chamber, revealing its features. The walls were decorated with a faded frieze, the ceiling was cobwebbed, the floor dusty. At the far end of the room was a stone altar or table, a band of carvings about its middle. A dark rectangle stood behind it. The strand at Pol's fingertips ran directly across the block of stone and vanished into the shadowy oblong.

Pol listened but heard nothing other than their own breathing.

He moved forward, Nora at his side, their footsteps muffled. For him, the air was alive with strands, as if they passed through a three-dimensional web woven of rainbows. Still, the milky green strand could not be lost. Eyes open or closed, he knew precisely where it hung.

They separated to pass around the altar, and Pol increased his pace to reach the small doorway first, duck his head and pass within, a mounting feeling of anticipation hinting at some climax beyond its threshold.

The light shot in before him and, on his willed command, rose to a level above his head and increased in brilliance.

This room was smaller than the outer one and it, too, possessed something resembling a low altar at its farther end. Flanking this was a pair of stone or stuffed jackals, eyes fixed forward. A great mass of the strands, all of them of the darker shades, were woven into strange patterns about the altar and the jackals. No doorway was visible behind this carved block, but rather a tall, shadowy figure, roughly man-shaped save for its head which resembled those of the jackals. Something small and glowing rested upon a dark green cushion atop the stone before it.

Pol swept his arm backward, halting Nora.

"What do you see?" he asked her.

"Another table and two statues," she said. "Something on the table . . ."

"According to the description and the sketch, that appears to be what I'm after," he said. "I want you to wait here while I go and try to take it. I expect to meet some sort of resistance and I'll probably have to improvise. All those braided areas look menacing."

"Braided areas? What do you mean?"

"There is some sort of spell protecting it. You stand guard while I find out what it does."

"Go ahead. I'm ready."

He took a single step forward. A pulse of light raced about the loops, the knotted junctions, leaping from figure to figure. He took a second step.

Hold, came a command he was certain that Nora could not hear. It seemed to beat upon him from the sudden vibrations of all the strands, passing down them from the shadowy figure behind the stone.

Why? he sent back immediately, deciding that it was no time to be shy.

He halted, to see what the reaction would be. The figure actually seemed to deliberate for a moment. Then, *You approach a thing I guard, presumably to remove it,* it replied. *I will not permit it.*

You refer to the section of rod on the stone before you?

That is correct.

I confess that I would like to have it. Does your charge permit you to make any sort of deal whatsoever for it?

No.

Pity. It would make life so much simpler for both of us.

I see that you are a young sorcerer, but recently come to the Art. If you were to live, you would probably become a great one. If you depart immediately, you will have that opportunity. I will let you go unmolested.

Pol took another step forward.

That is your answer?

I'm afraid so.

The jackal-headed figure raised its right arm, pointed a finger. The hovering dragon-light went dark. Pol felt a shock in his wrist. His vision seemed unimpaired, however, as if he viewed the chamber in the light of all the strands.

"Pol! What happened?" Nora cried.

"It's all right," he said. "Stay put."

He decided against resummoning the glowing image. That did not seem terribly imaginative, and it would probably just be put out again. It seemed that some measure of variety and originality should govern in these matters.

He sent the power that throbbed in his wrist out along the jade strand, causing the rod-section itself to begin glowing where it lay upon the table of stone. He pictured himself turning a lamp switch for a three-way light bulb, willing more wattage, raising the glow. The chamber brightened on a mundane level.

"Better?" he asked Nora.

"Yes. What is happening?"

"A conflict seems to have begun—with the forces which guard here. Hold on."

Young man, do you think you are the first to come here, to seek the rod?

The figure raised both arms, spreading them. The light Pol had summoned trebled in intensity. Dim forms, which he had taken for rubble—on the floor, in corners, near the statues—were suddenly clearly illuminated. He saw many strewn bones. He counted four skulls.

All those who came remained.

Pol felt his fingers twitch toward a yellow strand, but he suppressed the impulse to seize it. It drifted nearer. He knew that his magical sense was showing him a weapon, and for the first time he overrode it—his reason telling him that its employment had better be a matter of careful timing.

The strand doubled and redoubled, looping back upon itself, hovering near his shoulder.

Uh—is it possible, Pol inquired, edging forward, *simply to borrow it and bring it back later? I've an excellent guitar I could leave for security—*

This is not a pawnshop! I am a guardian and you are a thief!

That is not true. It belonged to my father.

There came another pulse of light, and the beast to his right and ahead began to move, slowly at first, taking a step toward him. The other blinked and twitched its ears.

Now it belongs here, came the reply.

Pol reached up and seized the bunched yellow strands. With a jerk and a burst of power that ran along his arm, he tore them down and back, then brought them forward like a lash across the face of the advancing beast. It snarled and cried, drawing back, and he struck again. The third time that he hit it, it cringed, lowering its belly to the floor. At that moment, he noticed that the second jackal was about to spring.

Even as he turned and drew back his arm, he realized that he would not be able to strike in time . . .

*   *   *

Moonbird's view of the west was partly blocked by the pyramid, so that he did not see the bird-things dark against the brilliant sky until their van was near. Several began to dive as he raised his head, but they pulled up sharply and continued on.

Then he saw the falling object, and superimposed upon it came the image out of his dream. He spread his wings immediately to take to the air.

By the time the bombs struck, he was fifteen meters above them and climbing. He felt the heat building within his stomachs. Above him, he counted eight of the fliers. Good, he acknowledged. He had been waiting for an opportunity to meet them when he was unencumbered with passengers.

The bright flames were faded to smoke beneath him. Above, the formation had already begun its turn. Extending his neck and plowing the sky with his wings, he rose to meet them.

*   *   *

. . . And as he turned to strike at the leaping form, Pol saw Nora's blade fall upon it—a two-handed, overhead blow that landed upon its right shoulder behind the neck. Crying out, the creature twisted, giving Pol the opportunity to sidestep and bring his magical whip lashing soundlessly down upon it.

He moved ahead and to the right as it fell, writhing, to the floor. The strands of his yellow weapon cut it again, across the face. Nora had withdrawn her blade and moved back to heft it for another swing . . .

Continuing his advance into a position very near to the altar, he brought his whip-arm out and around to deliver another, heavier blow . . .

He was almost pulled from his feet as the figure at the back of

the altar extended its arm and seized the falling strands that he
wielded. At that moment, it seemed that the ground shook beneath him.

The strands were torn from his grip as his momentum sent him
spinning, catching at the edge of the stony table. Realizing where
the fall was bearing him as he plunged before that awesome presence, and certain that its next move would be to extinguish his
life if he did not act immediately, he reached out with his right
hand and seized the section of rod that rested on the cushion
nearby. It responded with the immediate surge of energy he had
felt might be present, a force his new sensitivity recognized as
utilizable.

He turned the end of the rod upward the moment he caught
hold of it, channeling the power from its manifold connections
into a white, flame-like burst of power that shot against the
animal-headed figure's inclined breast.

No!

He saw it driven backward even as he slipped to the floor.
From his hand, the glow of the rod still illuminated the entire
chamber.

Rolling to the side, he saw that both jackals lay still nearby. He
felt Nora's hand take hold of his left arm, helping him to his feet.

"You're all right?"

"Yes. Yourself?"

"Yes."

He looked back. The strands still billowed about the stone, but
were now in total disarray, their patterns undone. The shadowy
figure was far dimmer but seemed in the process of reassembling
by attraction several portions of itself which had dispersed. He
held his new weapon before him and backed away, Nora at his
side.

When they reached the doorway to the next chamber, they
turned and fled through it. Rounding the altar, they continued on.
The air seemed much dustier here than it had been earlier. When
they had mounted the stair and were traversing the forward passageway, a crashing sound came to them from outside.

Racing toward the light, they emerged to view a crumpled flier beyond the first column to their left. There were two large craters ahead and to the right. One statue was upset and broken and a column had fallen across the way. Farther along, there were two more wrecked fliers.

Pol heard a sound from overhead and looked upward. There was nothing in view in the sky. Turning, he then saw that two more of the birds were shattered against the side of the pyramid. As he stared, another circled into and out of view above that mountain of stone. Since Moonbird was no longer where he had left him, he was not surprised, moments later, to see his great green and bronze form wheel into view over the top of the monument. Two of the fliers then came into sight, circling, diving at the dragon. As their positions continued to shift, Pol saw that there was a third. He thought, too, that he detected an occasional puff and the echo of a small report from the machines. If they did have guns, they at least did not appear to be rapid-fire automatic weapons. Their main tactic seemed to consist of darting attempts to slash at their larger, slower opponent with their spear-like beaks and the fore-edges of their wings. They were closing with him again even as Pol watched.

Not knowing what he might be able to do at this distance, he sought strands. They seemed to be everywhere, just awaiting the proper act of discernment and manipulation . . . Indeed! They became visible to him—an orange trail leading upward. He reached for them and they drifted toward him, along with an enormous feeling of separation and the formula for electrical resistance, which he had learned one summer while working for his stepfather. He took this as an indication that he was not going to be able to do much to help Moonbird. Then the rod-segment jerked in his hand and he wondered. He studied it for the first time in full light.

It was of a light, heavily tarnished metal—possibly an alloy of some sort; and if so, far too technologically sophisticated for anything he had seen here, save for Mark's creations—and this seemed old, felt old, as his special sense measured things. It was about eight inches long and opened at one end, presumably to accommodate the succeeding section; its other end was a simple hemisphere, possibly of a different metal. About the shaft itself was chased a pattern of stylized flames within which a rich variety of demons danced and engaged in peculiar acts.

He raised it—it seemed that it might be some sort of magical battery, or transformer—and, with a rapid twisting motion, he twined an orange strand about it. Nora, who had been about to speak, realized from his gesture and his intent expression that he was conjuring and she remained silent, eyes fixed upon the shaft.

Suddenly, the distance seemed telescoped, and he found himself working with the far end of the strand, weaving, looping, turning it into a wide net before a diving flier. To affect something of that mass and velocity, at that distance, he realized that an enormous amount of power would have to flow upward. He felt it go out of him as he willed it, and the rod jerked within his grip.

The flier sped into the trap he had attempted to lay, and it did not seem impeded by it. It rushed on toward Moonbird's flank, as Pol felt weak from willing energy into his snare.

Then, all at once, it veered crazily—one wing held high, the other low. It seemed frozen in that position, spinning ahead, slowing, in a dropping, drooping trajectory that bore it beneath the dragon, turning until it was headed downward. It rotated all the way to the ground, where it stopped. Even before it struck, another followed it, blazing, target of Moonbird's fiery regurgitations.

Pol turned his attention to the final flier, which suddenly seemed bent upon a suicide attack on the lazily turning sky-beast. He knew that no time remained for the slow knottings of another spell, and he doubted that from this distance he could release an effective blast such as that which had felled the guardian in the pyramid. And even as he raised the rod for the attempt, he saw the small white puff and moments later heard the report.

Moonbird showed no sign of having been hit, however, and as the bird-thing plunged toward him, he moved to meet it, twisting in a serpentine fashion, acquiring more speed than the moment seemed to offer. As they met, he clasped the flier to him and began his descent.

Nora and Pol watched him spiral downward in a leisurely fashion, coming to rest near the rim of a nearby crater, turning so as to land directly atop the captive flier with a series of crunching noises which ceased only when he moved away from the broken device, which a final nudge sent toppling and sliding into the hole.

Well-fought, great one, he said. *You were injured . . . ?*

Hardly at all. And dragons heal quickly. You have the thing you sought?

Yes. This is it.

He displayed the piece.

I have seen it before, joined with the others. Gather your things, come mount me and let us be on our way to wherever you would go now.

You should rest after such a struggle.

A dragon rests on the wing. Let us leave this place if we are finished here.

Pol turned to Nora.

"He is able to go on now. How about you?"

"I'd like to get out of here myself."

He looked at her for the first time in a long while. Dishevelled and moist with perspiration, she still clutched the blade in her right hand. But he saw no signs of injury.

Noting his regard, she relaxed her grip on the weapon and sheathed it. She smiled.

"All right?"

"All right. Yourself?"

He nodded.

"Then let's get our stuff together and move on. Have you any idea how he knew we'd be here?"

"No," she said. "You say that the things he does are not really magic—but they do seem that way to me. It's just that he has a different style."

"I hope you like my style better."

"So far," she said.

As Moonbird lifted them above the desert and bent his course northward, the skies were clear and the sun had already begun its western plunge.

Land where you would to forage, Pol told him. *Once we hit the northern sea, we'll be island-hopping—and the maps are not all that good on distances.*

I have been this way before, Moonbird told him. *I will feed in time. Now, will you make some music to warm my cold reptilian heart?*

Pol unearthed his guitar, tuned it and struck a chord. The wind whistled accompaniment as the land unrolled like a dry and mottled parchment beneath them.

XVII.

That night, as they lay listening to the sound of waves and breathing the smell of the sea on a small island far from the mainland, Moonbird sought sustenance far afield and Nora studied the rod from the pyramid.

"It does have a magical look, a magical feel to it," she said, turning it in the moonlight.

"It is that," Pol replied, stroking her shoulder, "and the other two pieces should do more than just add to its potency. Each should multiply the power of those which precede, several times."

She put it aside and reached out to touch his wrist.

"Your birthmark," she said. "They weren't really wrong—the villagers. You *are* of that tribe with your feet in hell and your head in heaven."

"No reason to throw rocks," he said. "I wasn't doing anything to them."

"They'd feared your father—once he got involved in blood sacrifices and the treating with unnatural beings who had to be paid in human lives."

Pol shrugged.

". . . And they took his life to balance accounts. Also, my mother's. And they wrecked the place. Didn't that pretty much square things?"

"At the time, yes—as I understand it. But you stirred up fears as well as leftover hatred. Supposing you'd come home to avenge their deaths? You did have that in mind, too, didn't you? That's what that Mouseglove person said."

"Not at the time, though. I hadn't even realized who I was when they attacked me. But it made it easier for me to hate them when I did learn."

"So, in a way they were right."

Pol took the rod into his hands and stared at it.

"I can't deny it," he said, finally. "But I didn't follow through on it. I've harmed none of them."

"Yet," she said.

He turned onto his side and glared at her, the covers slipping from his shoulder.

"What do you mean 'yet'? If I'd been that serious about it, it would have been my first order of business."

"But you still dislike them."

"Wouldn't you, in my position? So far as I'm concerned, they're not very likable people. And if they'd handled Mark a little differently, they probably wouldn't have him on their backs."

"They are quick to react to the unknown. Theirs is a settled way of life—traditional, slow to change. They saw both of you as threats to it and acted immediately to preserve it."

"Okay. I can see that. But I can understand something without liking it. I've called off the feud I almost declared on them. That should be enough."

"Only because you've got a bigger one on your hands. You know that if you don't destroy Mark he's going to destroy you."

"I have to operate under that assumption. He's given me every indication. The time is past for trying to talk with him."

She was silent for a long while.

"So why aren't you like the others?" he asked. "You were a friend of his and now you're hanging around with a dark sorcerer —helping me, in fact."

She remained silent. Then he realized that she was crying, softly.

"What is it?" he said.

"I'm a pawn," she answered in a low voice. "I'm the reason you got involved—you were trying to help me."

"Well—yes. But sooner or later Mark and I would have met, and the results would probably have been the same."

"I'm not so sure," she said. "He might have been more inclined to listen to you if it hadn't been for me. But he was jealous. You might have become friends—you have much in common. If you had— Think what an alliance that might have been—a sorcerer and a master of the old science arts—both out for revenge on my homeland. Now that cannot be, and the wheels are turning to bring you into a struggle to the death. Supposing I really hated you both? It wouldn't make a bit of difference—now."

"Do you?" he asked.

". . . And I'd be damned if I'd tell you."

"You wouldn't have to sleep with me. Once those wheels are in motion a roll in the hay wouldn't alter them."

"It might make the winner more disposed to leave us alone, out of a certain fondness."

"And telling him about it might have just the opposite effect."

"It's a good thing I'm talking principles and not cases," she replied, touching his shoulder again. "As I said, I do feel like a

pawn, though, and you wanted to know why. As for your last question, I was answering it as things could be, not informing you. It was the wrong question, anyhow."

"You're too tough to be a pawn," he said, "and you know who the only woman on the board is. And we can sleep with a sword between us if you want."

"It is not cold steel that I want," she said, moving nearer.

He saw a pale blue strand drifting by, but he ignored it.

Everything shouldn't be gimmicked, he thought. Should it?

*   *   *

He heard the voices again, in that place where he drifted between sleep and wakefulness.

"Mouseglove, Mouseglove, Mouseglove . . ."

Yes. It was not the first time he had heard them—weak yet insistent, calling to him—and on awakening he always forgot the small chorus. But this time there seemed more strength to the calls, almost as if he might come away with the memory, this time . . .

"Mouseglove!"

He began to remember his circumstances, sprawled in the secret apartment atop Anvil Mountain, unwilling guest of Mark Marakson, a.k.a. Dan Chain, taboo-breaking engineer from the east village. He was trying to find a way out, past the man's gnome-like legions and electronic spies, trying to learn to fly one of the small craft—small, yes, not like the battle-wagons with the six-man crews, two cannons and a rack of bombs he had seen take off earlier, sailing in every which direction across the sky, rotors whirling, wings tilting all about them—small, just right for himself and the jewelled figurines which would make him his fortune . . .

"Mouseglove!"

He was moved a jot and two tittles nearer awakening, yet still the chirping cries came to him. It was almost as if . . .

He tried. Suddenly, somewhere inside himself, he answered.

"Yes?"

"We bring warning."

"Who are you?"

Immediately, his dream-sight began to function. He seemed to stand at the center of a low-ceilinged room, illuminated by seven enormous candles. A figure, human in outline, stood behind each of them. The flames obscured the faces, and no matter how he turned or stared, nothing more of them was revealed to him.

"You sleep with the figures beneath your head," said the one at the extreme left—a woman's voice—and immediately he knew.

Four men, two women and one of uncertain gender, out of red metal, studded in peculiar places with jewels of many colors . . . Somehow, they addressed him now:

"We gained power when the Triangle of Int was unbalanced by the heir of Rondoval," said the second figure—a man.

"We are the spirits of sorcerers vanquished by Det and bound to his statuettes," said the third—a tall man.

"We exist now mainly to serve him or his successor," said the fourth—a woman with a beautiful soprano voice.

"We see futures and their likelihoods," said the fifth—a gruff-voiced man.

"We have come into your possession for a reason," said the sixth—of uncertain gender.

". . . For we can to some extent influence events," finished the man on the right—the seventh.

"What is your warning?" asked Mouseglove. "What do you want?"

"We see a great wave about to break upon this plane," said the first.

". . . At this place," said the second.

"Soon," said the third.

". . . To settle the future of this world for some time to come," said the fourth.

"Pol must be protected," said the fifth.

". . . At this point of the Triangle," said the sixth.

A map was lying before him on the floor. It was actually a part of the floor, he now realized, cunningly inscribed. It seemed that

it had been there all along. As he looked, one spot grew light upon it.

"Steal maps, steal weapons, take Mark's flier and go to that place," said the seventh.

"Take Mark's flier?" he asked.

"It is the fastest and is capable of the greatest range," said the first.

"Pol isn't a bad guy," Mouseglove said, "and I wish him no ill, but my intention is to get as far away from him and Mark as soon as I can, as fast as I can."

"Your willing cooperation would make things easier," said the second.

". . . But it is not absolutely necessary," said the third.

". . . As our power rises," said the fourth.

"I've never had booty talk back to me before," Mouseglove replied, "except for a parrot, when I was a lad. But that doesn't count. You're asking too much. I've led a dangerous life, but this was to be my last big risk. You are my retirement security. I want nothing to do with your breaking wave."

"Fool," said the fifth.

". . . To think you have a choice," said the sixth.

"You have walked a charmed line since the day you entered Rondoval," said the seventh.

"We had a part in everything that brought you to this point," said the first.

"Even our theft," said the second.

Mouseglove chuckled.

"If I have no choice, then why do you request my cooperation?" he asked. "No. Perhaps I was manipulated up to this point. Now, though, I think you need my help and your power has not risen sufficiently to insure it. I'll take my chances. The answer is no."

Silence followed. He felt himself the object of intense scrutiny.

Then, "You are shrewd," said the third, "but incorrect. The answer is merely that it would be easier for us with your cooperation. We could devote our energies to other matters than your coercion."

"We can see that you are suitably rewarded," said the fourth.

"Rewards are of no benefit to a dead man," he stated. "No deal."

"You will not like what Mark does to this world," said the fifth.

"I've never been totally happy with it the way that it is," he replied. "But I get by."

"For your own protection then, learn to use the grenades. They practice with them on the southern rim," said the sixth, neutral-voiced.

". . . And get the maps," said the seventh.

"That much I intended anyway," Mouseglove answered. "But I am not going to the place you showed me and do any fighting there."

The candles flickered, the room expanded toward nothingness and his consciousness faded. The last thing that he heard was the sound of their voices, laughing.

* * *

Three flying boats approached Castle Rondoval cautiously, guns loaded and swiveling in pace with the vessels' circling movements. As the circles diminished, the first battle-wagon discharged a shot across the battlements. At this point, all three were poised to withdraw and regroup in the face of a severe reaction. Nothing, however, followed.

The circling continued for the better part of an hour, though no more shots were fired. Finally, the vessels—very close, very low now—broke formation to drift about among the still-standing towers, to hover while their occupants peered through windows and damage gaps in the walls. Slowly, then, one of the three floated to a landing in the main courtyard. None of its occupants emerged immediately, and the other two ships moved above it, guns ready. A quarter of an hour passed, and nothing stirred but the leaves on the trees and a lizard on the wall.

At last, a large hatch at the rear fell open and five small figures emerged, weapons held ready, to rush for cover in five different directions, dropping to earth and remaining motionless as soon as it was achieved. After several minutes, they rose and began to move, entering the castle.

It was over an hour before they emerged, their attitudes more casual, their weapons slung. Their leader signalled to the other two vessels, which immediately began to descend. When they were down, five more individuals emerged from each of them.

The fifteen men stood about, conferring on the building's layout. At last, they returned to the vessels to bring forth heavier weapons for emplacement inside.

Later that afternoon, when Rondoval had been secured, one of the vessels departed, leaving behind a dozen men, one on permanent duty in each of the remaining ships, the other ten set to patrol the castle.

The departing battle-wagon spiraled outward, moving more rapidly than on its inward journey, ship's telescope sweeping the rocky heights and, finally, the forested depths of the vicinity. Still, it was nearly an hour before a small group of centaurs was detected in a distant glade.

The sky boat dropped immediately to a point near treetop-level, out of line of sight of the creatures. It descended into the first clear area it reached, where its engines died and its hatch opened. The five infantrymen emerged, moving away into the trees, the pilot remaining behind with the vessel.

They passed slowly and silently through the forest, having spent basically predatory existences before their present level of culture had been thrust upon them. Now they fanned, like a well-organized hunting team, moving to surround their prey. As they neared the glade, they communicated entirely by a kind of sign language, messages passing from man to man about the circle they formed. Taking up their positions, they studied the disposition of the eight centaurs in the area and commenced a rapid and elaborate sign discussion as to target assignments. Then they raised their weapons.

The signal was then passed, and each of the five fired one round. Five centaurs jerked and bled. Two fell immediately. None of the riflemen paused to reload his single-shot weapon. Instead, they rushed forward to use the butts as clubs, only two finally drawing the blades they wore at their sides. There were only a few cries from the centaurs, but the smells of sweat and urine were suddenly strong upon the air.

One of the wounded ones rose unexpectedly, crushing an attacker's skull with her forehoofs. She was beaten down along with the three unwounded. The lightest of the uninjured had his legs bound together and hands tied behind him. Three of the remaining attackers slung their weapons and moved to transport him, the fourth reloading and covering them.

They bore their burden back through the woods, encountering no resistance. They entered and secured the vessel. Shortly thereafter, the rotors became shimmering blurs and the ship rose slowly, took its course and drifted southward, acquiring altitude, its speed slowly mounting as it passed above the deepening forest.

*　*　*

Moonbird flew above the dark, convoluted patterning—a large, flat design within the field of rock—at the other end of the long island from the city and its ports. Shadows cast by the morning's sun broke the scheme in numerous places, and the entire prospect caused a swimming effect whenever one stared for too long. Pol gestured as if to interrupt his vision, for countless dark strands now drifted from it, further blurring, confusing the image.

Some power lies there, beneath the ground, Moonbird remarked. *This is the place?*

Yes.

Pol scanned the skies carefully, then looked down once again. There was one break, at the pattern's northern edge, where the strands billowed like an inkpot dropped into an aquarium.

Take us down at that far end, where the stand of trees comes in like a spearpoint, nearest to the thing.

Moonbird slowed and began his descent. Pol strained forward, studying the terrain. Soon, he saw that the marked area was an elaborate, monolithic construction, the dark lines representing a continuous overhead opening, presumably running the entire length of many interconnected interior corridors for purposes of some small illumination. The structure itself stood perhaps twice his height above ground level. As they slowed to land, Pol saw the single pale jade strand he sought among the masses of sable and ochre lines. A faint bellowing noise reached his ears from some undeterminable point.

As he touched the ground, Moonbird asked:

Play me one more song.

Do you fear that you will never hear one again?

Humor an old sauroid servitor. Dragons have their reasons.

Very well.

Pol uncased his guitar, not even bothering to dismount.

"What are you doing?" Nora inquired.

"Request performance," he answered, and he began a long, slow, nostalgic ballad.

Thank you, Moonbird replied, when it was finally concluded.

*That was soothing, and you reminded me of a story that a griffin
once told me—*

*I'm afraid that I do not have the time to hear it now. More of
those metal birds with bombs could—*

Did you notice anything special as you sang?

No. What do you mean?

The bellowing sounds. They stopped.

Pol climbed down and assisted Nora in alighting. He patted
Moonbird's neck.

Thanks.

"How do you intend to approach this one?" Nora asked. "The
same way as . . ."

She had barely noticed the twirling motion of Pol's left hand,
two fingers extended, slightly bent. As they moved near to her
face, it felt as if a black bandage were sliding across her eyes . . .

Pol caught her as she slumped, bearing her to a spot beneath
the branches of the nearby trees, largely sheltered from overhead
view.

Guard her while I'm inside, he told Moonbird. *If more of those
things show up, it would be better if you stay hidden here for so
long as you are undetected.*

I can break them.

*But then Nora will be unprotected. No. Only fight if you are
discovered.*

Moonbird snorted and drops of spittle fell upon the ground and
began to smolder.

Very well. I can at least listen to the music.

Pol turned away and approached the high, wide entrance. A
snuffling, growling sound commenced somewhere within—distant
or near, he could not be certain. It shifted about him, moving,
growing, diminishing.

The corridor he had entered ended abruptly several paces before him. There was a lower, narrower opening to his right and
the strand led directly into it.

He halted and hung the guitar by its strap. He began to play, a
slow, lullaby-like tune, into which he poured a wrist-throbbing

desire to calm, to charm any listener. Several strands drifted near and he caught them on the neck of the instrument and saw them grow taut and begin to pulse in time with the music.

Slowly, he turned, still playing, and entered the opening.

He found himself in a dim passageway, a narrow band of sky visible high above him, running like a blue brook to separate into several tributaries at a place where a number of corridors met. He stood still for a time, strumming and humming, letting his eyes adjust to the lesser light. He realized then that the snorts and snufflings had ceased, though there was now a sound of heavy breathing all about him.

He moved forward, following the pale green strand. He turned right when it did, and left and immediately left again. Two more paces bore him into a circular chamber, ten equidistant doorways in its walls, including the one from which he had just emerged.

His strand led through the one to the immediate right, though another section of it crossed the chamber, stretched between two other doors. He ignored this and followed it to the right.

There came a series of left-right, left-right, then left-left, right-right turns which left him dizzy. He paused to regain control of his music. The sounds of breathing still came heavily about him, filling all the passageways, accompanied now by a strong barn-yard odor. A tiny bit of cloud drifted across the blue band above him. Switching to another tune—still languid, dreamlike—he continued on.

After a time, he entered a circular chamber with ten doors, fol-lowing the strand across it. He felt that it was the same one through which he had passed earlier, because of a familiar pattern of cracks in the wall, but there was no trace of the green strand passing between the adjacent doors across the way.

Then, looking behind him, he realized that the jade strand was shrinking or being gathered before him as he progressed. It was then that it occurred to him that while the force within the object he sought made it easy to describe a spell that would lead him to it, finding his way back out again might be a little more difficult without such a goal.

He ducked and squatted as he traversed a low passage—hell of

a place to get caught!—and turned sideways as he negotiated a
narrow one. He then entered upon a fresh series of turns, most of
them doubling back upon themselves.

How long? he wondered. Surely I don't have to go through the
entire thing . . .

Shortly thereafter, he realized that the breathing sounds had
grown louder. And it was not long after that that he entered the
long, low hall where the minataur paced . . .

* * *

Mouseglove leaned forward again. The light in Mark's penthouse had been out for the better part of an hour, yet he had
learned by observation that the sometime flashing device which
had replaced the man's left eye was capable of very effective
night-vision. He was also aware of Mark's restless disposition, of
his inclination to pace within his quarters, to burst suddenly forth
and embark upon surprise inspections of his installations, his factories, the barracks, his laboratories, his fields.

Is it better to assume that sleep has claimed him? he wondered.
He's had a busy day. Still, he's so full of nervous energy . . . He
could come out at any time. Once he's off and running again, it
would be easy . . .

More maps than he really needed were folded in the various
pockets of his cloak. The package containing the seven figurines
was there, also. The grenades—about which he felt even more
uncomfortable, having earlier witnessed their power—hung from
his belt, along with one of his daggers. He carried a parcel containing food and a pistol he had stolen.

He leaned back behind the duct again and breathed more
deeply of the chill and smoky night air. The longer he waited, of
course, the greater the risk of discovery by one of the gnomes or
machines. He was certain that he had spotted all of the stationary
alarm devices, yet there were mobile units.

Still, he realized that he could not enter the flier and secure it
about him without making some noise. Even if Mark were al-

ready sleeping, it would be well to let him drift further along into oblivion.

He looked up at the stars. The moon had not risen. Good for stealth. Less good for one's first flight. He touched each grenade. He checked his supplies. He had no intention of being captured. Especially after having seen what they had done to that centaur they had brought in earlier. And he was convinced that the poor

brute had not even understood what it was that they wanted to know.

Patience had long been a way of life with Mouseglove. He commenced massaging major muscles, pausing periodically to listen, to peer about him.

Over an hour went by.

Time, he decided. The belly of the night. Two hundred paces now. Slow and steady. Patron of Thieves, be with me . . .

It was time to think of nothing, to be an eye, to be an ear, to breathe just so, to feel vibrations. The hatch *would* have to be on the side facing Mark's door . . .

Twenty more paces, ten . . . What are they burning in those factories, anyway? It bites the nose . . .

He circled the vehicle twice, seeking alarms. Finally, he extended his hand, touched the smooth, cold body of the ship . . .

Now, little man, there is no retreat, he told himself.

He cracked the hatch, drawing slowly and steadily upon it. Silently, it came open. A moment later, he was inside, scanning the rooftop, seeking the hatch's interior handle. There would be an unavoidable noise in closing it. He located the handle and pulled downward upon it until it was only opened a crack . . .

No!

The door to Mark's apartment banged open and the man himself emerged. Mouseglove's fingers outlined and dug for the pistol within his parcel on the seat beside him. There was not time in which he might take off, no way in which he could flee.

Yet, Mark did not immediately advance. He stood with his thumbs hooked behind his belt, studying the sky, the roof. Could it be that it was only the man's insomnia which had brought him outside?

Mouseglove realized that he was holding his breath. He let it out slowly and took the pistol onto his lap. His left arm was beginning to tremble, from holding the door nearly closed against the tension of its spring.

. . . And don't let it rattle, he appended to his latest prayer.

He located the trigger and raised the pistol. Abruptly, Mark buttoned his jacket and closed the door behind him. He began walking across the terrace.

I'd shoot him. Right now. If I could be sure of getting him. But I've never used one of these things. And already my grip is slippery upon it. I'd take the chance with a crossbow, if I had one. If this door were shut and the window down . . . If . . .

Mark passed within five meters, without even glancing at the flier. Mouseglove, deep within his cowl, crouched, arm aching, watched him go.

It was another ten minutes before he dared to slam the hatch and turn his attention to the controls.

*   *   *

Pol did not permit the music to falter. The man-beast's eyes had passed over him several times as it moved slowly back and forth along the hall. It was well over two meters tall, with dark, curved horns. The room stank. Pol wondered what sort of teeth the creature possessed, with the head of a herbivore and the reputation he was still fresh on from his recent readings. He decided that he was willing to leave the question to sorcerers of a more academic bent. He turned his full attention to his playing.

Only his hands moved. He imagined that he plucked strands extending from the instrument to the horns of the beast. The force that grew within his wrist seemed to flow out through his fingertips, into the guitar, across the distance that lay between them.

. . . *Rest. A nervous life such as yours requires some interlude of peace,* he sent within the song. *Not merely sleep, but the deep, muscle-easing joy of total rest that is almost pain, it is so sweet . . .*

The minotaur slowed even more, finally coming to a standstill beside the wall. Even its awful breathing slowed.

. . . *Forget, forget the moment. The dream-sights dance already behind eyes that would close. Approach the cloud-strewn border of the land where visions dwell. They beckon . . .*

The minotaur put out his right hand and leaned upon the wall. His head nodded. He snorted softly, once.

. . . Go, go to that place. There, skiey towers caressed by cool breezes make sweet the forgetting—and in fields of flowing green you wander. Delight spills across your body like a gentle rain. You bathe in the pools of healing. Bright colors fill your vision. There comes a song that brings you peace . . .

The creature knelt, lowered himself to the floor. His eyes closed.

Pol continued to play for a long while. There was little expression upon that sleeping face, other than a certain slackness. And the minotaur's breathing had grown much slower and quieter. For the first time, Pol dared to look away from him, to trace with his eyes the path of the strand he had followed.

The green line led to a niche, high in the wall at the far end of the room. There were several clusterings of the darker strands about it, but these were far less elaborate than those he had encountered beneath the pyramid—and apparently cast where they were mainly for purposes of protecting the faintly glowing cylinder from molestation by the minotaur himself.

Pol moved quietly across the stone floor in that direction, his hands automatically continuing the melody as he studied the knottings of the spells. There were three of them, any one of which might have stopped the minotaur or an ordinary man. Yet, their undoing should take a competent sorcerer no more than—

He glanced back at the sleeping creature as he realized that he would have to stop playing in order to unwind the spells.

He reduced the tempo and strummed more softly.

. . . *Sleep, sleep, sleep* . . .

He stopped and lowered the instrument. His left hand twisted forward. When the first spell was undone, he glanced back and saw that the beast still slumbered.

As he worked on the second one, he heard a noise behind him, but at that moment he could not look away. Finally, it fell apart beneath his hands and he turned quickly, strands dispersing all about him.

The minotaur had only turned in its sleep.

He returned to the consideration of the final spell. It was no more difficult than the others. But he could not rush its untwining, for the proper pace was as much a matter of necessity as the appropriate movements. His left hand darted, hooked and twisted. These last strands were colder than the others and, correspondingly, released a greater feeling of heat when they were at last undone.

Again, Pol looked back.

The minotaur's eyes were open and staring at him.

Who are you?

A singer.

What do you want here?

A mere bauble.

The thing in the niche? It bites. Take care.

I shall. You do not mind that I take it?

Why should I? It is nothing to me. Where have I been?

Dreaming.

I had never been there before. There were bright things I'd never seen . . .

Colors?

Perhaps. Everything was good. Like never before. I want to go there again.

That can be arranged.

I want to dwell there forever.

Close your eyes then, and listen to the music.

The minotaur closed his eyes.

Bring this music and send me away . . .

Pol began to play, recovering all the visions which had come to him earlier. As he did, his eyes passed over the second section of the rod in its niche—longer, narrower than the first segment, bearing a scene of animals and men and woodland spirits, free of strife, dancing, eating, loving . . .

He struck the strings, reached out, seized the rod-section and fitted it into the first at his belt. Then he resumed playing, as the minotaur still drowsed. He felt the increased warmth, the mightily enhanced sense of power that now twisted about the rod. As he played, he called upon it for a new usage and he felt that power move warmly through his abdomen, down his arm, into the guitar, to be joined with the music itself.

. . . Across the fields, where there is no strife, no hunger, no pain, where no one is a monster, where the light is soft, where the birds call and the brooks burble, where twilight comes on bringing stars like swarms of fireflies—to dwell there forever, never to awaken, never to depart—sleep, bullman, in the peace you had never known—always, ever . . .

Pol turned away from the sleeper. He touched his wrist to the new section of the rod. Somewhere, buried in his unconscious, it seemed that there should be a record of every step, every turning he had taken on the way in. Therefore—

The dragon-image rose like a phoenix glowing above his wrist. Surely, it should be able to reach those buried memories.

Go! he commanded. *I follow!*

It darted away from him, to depart the hall from the doorway nearest the niche, rather than the one through which he had entered.

He hesitated only a moment, then followed, smiling. So much for theory. He took it as a message that the forces his special sense reached and manipulated were not to be categorized in so facile a manner.

As he took his first turn beyond the doorway, he had his final glimpse of the sleeping minotaur, over his right shoulder. He saw the knot of his own spell drifting above the prostrate form, like a giant, yellow butterfly.

* * *

Mouseglove's relief was immense as the ship cleared the highest tower and soared out, away from Anvil Mountain. Already, the lights of its city were small beneath him, and he was surprised to be taken by a sensation of beauty viewed as he looked upon it. Turning away, he continued to direct the vessel up past the regions where the dark bird-things wove their interminable patterns. So far, there was no indication of pursuit. He pushed the ship to its ultimate speed and held it there until the mountain was only a dim outline behind him. At last, this, too, faded and only the stars gave him light.

Then he relaxed, unclasping his cloak and letting it fall over the back of his seat. He sighed and rubbed his eyes and ran his fingers through his hair. A great tension began draining away, and the beginnings of delight in the act of flying under his own control came over him.

Soon . . . At this speed, he would be in Dibna before morning. That would provide ample time for hiding the vessel and walking into town. In a day's time, he should be able to locate a buyer or a middle-man for the disposition of the figurines. A few days more, possibly, to tie up the deal. Then, his purse full of coins, he would treat himself to a bit of revelry. After that, use the flying machine to travel to another town where no one would know of the transaction. In fact, it might be best to do that before celebrating. Then find a place to settle down. A villa on a hillside, with a view of the sea. A cook, a manservant, a gardener—it would be pleasant to have a garden—and a few assorted slave girls . . .

He turned the control wheel slowly to the right. More, more . . . Southeast, south . . . He began to wonder why he was doing it. This was no longer the way to Dibna. He struggled to halt the motion, but his hands continued to move the control. Southwest . . . He was almost completely turned around. It would simply have to be corrected. Only . . .

His hands refused to obey, to turn him back. It was as if the will of another now directed his actions. He fought against it, but to no avail. He was now headed in almost exactly the one direction that he did not wish to go. As he watched himself being directed, the entire sequence of his actions took on a dreamlike quality, as though he himself were being forced further and further into the background, as though . . .

Dreamlike. For a moment, the tiny control lights swam before him, rearranging themselves into seven flickering forms. The full memory of his dream crashed down upon him then, with a feeling that somewhere the last laughter continued.

He had a strong premonition that he was saying good-bye to his villa.

* * *

Pol's first impulse on reaching the labyrinth's exit was to rush out through it. Instead, he halted just within the doorway. Something—he was not certain what—was amiss. It was as if he had been granted such a brief glimpse of a danger that he could not name it, could only be aware of its existence. Had something moved?

He wondered, looking out to the place where Moonbird watched a sleeping Nora. He took the rod into his hands and tried to recall elaborate spells from the books he had read in his father's collection. Everything seemed to be all right, yet . . .

A slow-moving shadow slid across the ground before him, twisting itself over every irregularity. Still, it was easy for him, coming from the world that he had, to recognize the outline as that of a flying machine—a thing larger than the dark birds, if the sound which now reached his ears were any indication of its nearness.

There was a partial spell he had studied, simpler than the complete version of the same thing. It might require considerable energy, but then, he need no longer work solely with his hands upon the fabric of reality . . .

He raised the rod and began moving it about him, catching and swirling large quantities of the strands, of every color. As the shadow receded, the clot of strands grew before him, assuming a disc-like shape. The colors drained from it as it spun and increased in diameter, until, at length, it was a shimmering shield larger than himself. Objects beyond it rippled and swam and the rod vibrated steadily, silently within his grip.

Now. He took a step forward and the shield advanced a similar distance. Its size seemed sufficient for its purpose and he slowed the swirling movement to restrict its growth, to maintain it at its present size.

The shadow had passed away to his left, and he moved the rod in that direction and tilted it upward. He took another step and scanned the sky carefully. Unlike the complete spell, which rendered its caster entirely invisible, the partial spell he had been able to weave created only a flat screen, capable of blocking observation from a single direction.

Another step, and he caught sight of the battle-wagon, swinging away, farther to the left. Turning sideways, he adjusted the shield and began walking toward the trees. If he were to remain stationary, there was a way to rest his arm. As it was . . .

He crossed the cleared area, turning to follow the movement of the vessel, like some negative-petalled flower after an anti-sun, distorting the light that fell upon it, until finally he was walking backward when he reached the trees.

Standing now before the tree of the girl and the dragon, he spun the shield larger, watching the wavering image of the circling battle-wagon through the upper righthand quadrant of the screen.

He reached out and touched Moonbird.

I am going to awaken her now, he indicated. *When I do, we are going to retreat within the wood.*

And not fight?

We may not have to.

I could barf it to ruin . . .

Not if it gets you first. Trust me.

He turned to Nora and began releasing her from the sleep-spell, reflecting on how much simpler things would have been

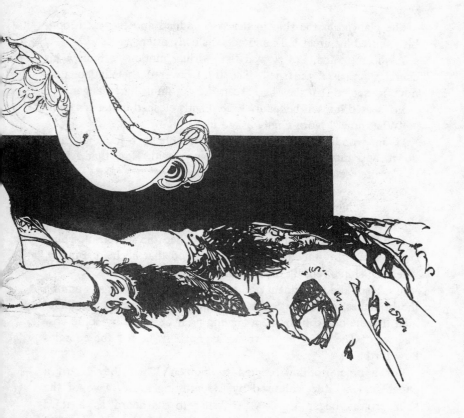

with the minotaur had he been able to do it at other than close range. Nora stirred, looked at him.

"I've been asleep! You did it to me! I—"

"Shh!" he cautioned. "They're up there!" He gestured with his head. "Sounds carry in a quiet place like this. Save it for later. I've got the second piece. Now we have to get off into the trees. We're invisible from just this one side."

She got to her feet and stood stiffly erect.

"It was not a nice trick," she said, "and you won't catch me that way again."

"I'll bear that in mind," he stated. "Now let's head back that way."

She glanced at the ship in the sky, nodded and turned. Moonbird shifted his great bulk and edged slowly after her.

As he retreated, Pol slowed the swirling motion, withdrew his energies, released the spell. The trees covered them adequately now. It seemed that they had escaped from immediate danger.

Pol seated himself beneath a tree, hands clasped under his chin.

"What now?" Nora finally asked him.

"I am wondering whether I might be able to bring that thing down, as I did that lesser one at the pyramid. Now that I have two of the sections together, it seems possible."

"It sounds worth trying."

"I am going to wait until its course brings it nearer. Distance does seem to be a factor."

For over a quarter of an hour, he watched the vessel, attaching strand after gray metallic strand to the rod that he held. Finally, when the ship swept by them again, he felt ready.

He raised the instrument and stared past it through gaps among the branches, amid the leaves, saw the strands grow taut, imagined that he could hear them singing as if caressed by some cosmic wind. The rod grew warm in his hand as he felt the energies flow forth.

For a time, nothing seemed to happen. Then they heard a cough and a rattle, followed by a sputtering noise. Two of the ship's rotors began to slow. It listed to starboard as a third propellor went out. Immediately, it began to descend, and Pol guessed that this was an action of the pilot's in trying to avoid a crash, rather than an indication that it might not remain airborne awhile longer. His knuckles grew white as he gripped the rod, willing more force into his spell. More rattling and coughing noises came from the sinking vessel. A thin wisp of smoke arose from beneath the cowling at its forward end. Two more rotors halted, but by now it was only fifteen or twenty meters above the ground, near to the western perimeter of the labyrinth.

It dropped only a short distance, moments later, and a hatch at its rear fell open. Three men hurried out and another followed more slowly, coughing. Pol saw a darting of flames within and more moving forms beating at and attempting to smother them. He lowered the rod and extended his hand to Nora.

"Let's get out of here," he said. "I've burned out several engines. They won't be able to follow."

They clambered up onto Moonbird's back.

Now! Hurry! Take us away!

We can finish them off first.

They are helpless now. Get us aloft!

Moonbird began a waddling run beneath the trees, fanning the air with his wings. When he broke into the cleared area, he lifted above the ground. A cry came up from somewhere to the right.

Pol saw the three men who had fled the smoldering battle-wagon. They were kneeling and had raised their weapons. White puffs emerged from the muzzles, and he immediately felt a burning pain in the back of his neck and slumped across Moonbird's shoulder. He heard Nora cry out and felt her catching at his shirt, his belt. His head swirled through dark places, but he did not immediately lose consciousness. A distant booming sound came to his ears. His neck was wet.

We should have finished them first . . . Moonbird was saying.

Nora was talking as she did something behind him, but he could not hear the words.

Then his eyes closed and everything diminished.

When the world came back, her hand was on his neck, holding a cold compress in place. He smelled the sea. He felt the play of muscles beneath the scales against which his cheek was pressed. Moonbird smelled a bit like old leather, gunpowder and lemon juice, he suddenly realized. Somehow the thought struck him as funny and he chuckled.

"You're awake?" said Nora.

"Yes. How serious is it?"

"It looks as if someone laid a hot poker across your neck and held it there for a time."

"That's about how it feels, too. What's on it?"

"A piece of cloth I soaked in water."

"Thanks. It helps."

"Do you know a spell to heal it?"

"Not offhand. But I may be able to think of something. Tell me first what happened, though."

"You were hit by something. I think it might have come from one of those smoking sticks the men were pointing."

"Yes, it did. But what was the crashing noise? Did their ship explode?"

"No. It had larger—things—like those pointed by the men. These turned to follow us, then they began smoking and making the noise. Several things seemed to explode near us. Then it stopped."

Pol propped himself and looked back. It hurt to turn his head. The island was already receding in the distance, its outline vaguely misted. He looked down at the sea, up toward the sun.

Moonbird, are you all right?

Yes. And you?

I'll be okay. But we seem to be heading northwest, rather than southwest. Maybe I'm wrong, though. You are the expert.

You are not wrong.

"Let me tie that in place for you."

"Go ahead."

Why? What is the matter?

The place you wish to visit next—it lies a great distance from here, many days' travel.

Yes, I know. That is why it is important that we follow the route I have laid out. Many island stopovers will be necessary.

Not really. Maps mean less to me than my feelings. I realized recently there is a shortcut.

How can that be? The shortest distance between two points is a—a great circle segment.

I will take us the way of the dragons.

The way of the dragons? What do you mean?

I have been that way before. Between some places there are special routes. Holes in the air, we call them. They move about, slowly. The closest one to a place near where you would go now lies in this direction.

Holes in the air? What are they like?

Uncomfortable. But I know the way.

Anything that is uncomfortable to a dragon might prove fatal to anyone else.

I have borne your father through them.

They are much faster?

Yes.

All right. Go ahead.

How far is it?

I may get us there by evening.

Is there a place before that where we can stop for repairs?

Several.

Good.

The sun hung low and red before them. To the right, a fuzzy line of coast darkened the horizon like a rough brush stroke. Mounds and streamers of pink and orange clouds filled the sky to the left and ahead. Moonbird was climbing and the wind seemed to grow colder with each beat of his wings. Pol stared upward and rubbed his eyes, for his vision had suddenly blurred.

The blur remained. He moved his head and it stayed in the same place.

Moonbird . . . ?

Yes, we are nearing it. It will be soon now.

Is there anything special that we should do?

Do not let go. Mind your possessions. I cannot help you if we become separated.

The wrinkle in the sky had grown larger as they climbed, reminding Pol of the invisibility shield viewed from the user's side. They reached its altitude and passed it. Looking down upon it, he saw it to be silvery, shining and opaque, like a pool of mercury, touched faintly pink by the receding sun. It achieved an even more substantial appearance as they rose higher above it.

Why have we passed it?

It must be entered from the bright side.

"We are going to dive through that?" Nora asked.

"Yes."

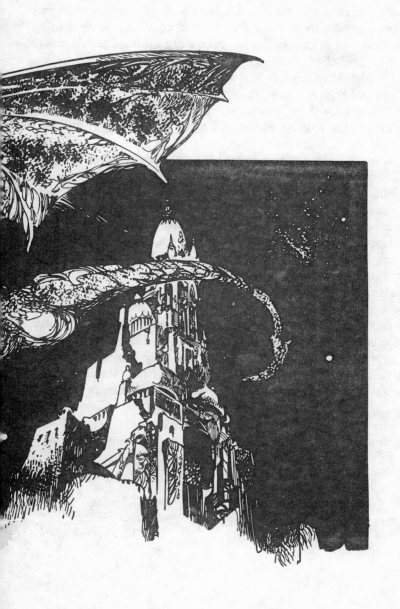

Pol touched the back of his neck and felt only a moderate ache. Already, the healing spell he had concocted seemed to be working—or at least killing the pain. Nora squeezed his shoulder.

"I'm ready."

He patted her hand as Moonbird achieved a position above the circle and began to slow.

"Hang on."

They began to drop. Moonbird's wings beat again, driving them faster.

It is not solid, Pol told himself without conviction, as the shining thing grew before them.

Suddenly, they were past it, and there was no up or down, only forward. Right and left would not stay put, for they seemed to be swirling, spiraling about a light-streaked vortex while a continuously rising scream pierced their ears. Pol bit his lip and clung tightly to Moonbird's neck. Nora was hugging him so hard that it hurt. He tried closing his eyes, but that worsened things, making his rising vertigo near to unbearable. There did seem to be a bit of brightness far, far ahead. His stomach wrenched, and whatever emerged was mercifully whipped away. Moonbird began expelling flames which fled back past them like glowing spears. The wailing had now reached at least partially into the ultrasonic. If he stared too long at the smears of light they seemed on the verge of becoming grotesque, open-mouthed faces. The one steady patch of brightness seemed no nearer.

Are all of the shortcuts like this? Pol asked.

No. We're lucky, Moonbird replied. *There are some bad ones.*

XVIII.

Eyes aching, shoulders sore from the long flight, Mouseglove circled the tumbling stone structure, saw no sign of other visitors and was about to land nearby. His hands jerked, however, swinging the vessel out over the jungle until a cleared area came into sight. His sigh was voluntary as he brought the small ship down for a landing, but when he attempted to utter a choice from his amazing collection of curses, he discovered that his tongue would not respond.

You could at least let me rest, he mentally addressed his unseen manipulators. *Whatever it is that you want of me, you will get a better performance if I am not exhausted.*

We regret the inconvenience, came their first communication since his dream on Anvil Mountain, accompanied briefly by a peculiar doubling of vision, as if the scene about him were momentarily overlaid by the image of a flickering taper, a dark presence moving near it. *But there is no choice. You overtook the other vessels during the night. We gave you a different course, and yours is a faster ship. But your lead is not that great. There is no time to rest. Take the wide, flat blade from the sheath on the door. Go outside. Cut branches, fronds. Conceal this vessel.*

He felt free—free to comply. He did not.

But—

He was seized once again. He felt himself begin to rise, springing the hatch, taking the blade into his hand. There were no replies to his next inquiries.

The great-leaved plants were easy to cut. It did not take him long to cover the small ship. Then he opened a compartment toward the vessel's rear, to strip it, clean it and snap auxiliary fuel cubes into its chambers. The thought of this situation had troubled him during a more alert moment. There was no way the sunlight converters could do the entire job required for the return trip, even if his unwilling hands had not covered over their panels with leaves.

When he had finished the work he stood still for a moment, breathing the warm moist air, listening to the morning calls of the

bright parrots, wondering whether he would now be permitted a brief rest. Almost as he thought it, however, his feet began to move, bearing him in what he believed to be the direction of the stone structure with the grotesque carvings. He swung the blade as he went, widening the trail. After only a few paces, he was drenched with perspiration. Insects buzzed about him, and the most maddening part of the entire experience was his inability to brush them away.

At last, he staggered into the cleared area where the stepped structure stood, stylized stone beasts projecting from its vine-covered walls, grinning past him.

I must rest, he tried. *In the shade. Please!*

There is absolutely no time, came the reply, with another flickering image. *You must go around to the other side of the building and enter there.*

He felt himself beginning to move again. He wanted to cry out, but this was still denied him. He moved faster and faster, barely aware of where he stepped, yet somehow he did not stumble.

He was halted again, before the weed-clogged, vine-hung doorway. Then the blade flashed forward and he began clearing it.

Soon he was through the opening and rushing along a corridor. His eyes had not yet adjusted to the gloom, but whatever was in charge of him seemed to know where he was going.

It was only when he neared the head of a wide flight of stairs that he began to slow, finally coming to a halt to regard the scene that lay below and before him, partly illuminated through an irregular gap in the roof where several stone blocks had fallen—the result of an earthquake perhaps . . .

At the far side of the chamber below was a low stone wall. Beyond it was the blackness of a hole. Before it was a diminutive version of the entire stepped building itself, complete with tiny statues and carvings. Atop this, in a crumbling orange basket, lay a narrow cylinder half the length of a man's forearm. It appeared to be glowing with a faint, greenish light. Mouseglove took advantage of the respite to breathe deeply of the moist air, to enjoy the coolness . . .

That, thief, is the object you must steal.

Again, the candle; again, the imperative.

The cylinder?

Yes.

Why bother to tell me? You're pulling all the strings.

Not any longer. We are about to release you. Your native wit and reflexes are superior to anything we might compel you to in such matters.

Suddenly, he was free. He mopped his brow, dusted his garments and fell to his knees, breathing heavily. One of his reflexes kept him silent, if this were indeed to be a piece of work. Mentally, he framed his most immediate question:

What is so difficult about descending these stairs, crossing the room and picking that thing up?

The dweller in the well.

What is it? What can it do?

If it detects your presence it will rise up and attempt to prevent the theft. It is a great feathered serpent.

Mouseglove began to shake. With his cloak, he muffled the lowering of the blade to the stone floor. He covered his face with his hands and rubbed his eyes, massaged his forehead.

This is so unfair! I only work in prime form, not when I'm half-dead with fatigue!

This time, there is no other way.

Damn you!

We are wasting time. Will you do it?

Have I any real choice? If there is any justice—

Then be about it!

Mouseglove dropped his hands and straightened. He swung into a seated position upon the top step and adjusted his boots. He ran his fingers through his hair, wiped his palms on his trousers and took up the blade. He stood.

With a silent, sweeping movement, he took himself to the lefthand side of the stair. Turning sideways then, he began to descend a step at a time, slowly and soundlessly.

When he reached the bottom, he stood perfectly still, listening. Was that the slightest of rustling noises from the well? Yes. It came again, then ceased. Would it be better to dash forward,

seize the cylinder and run for it now? Or should he continue to
rely on stealth? How big was the creature, and how fast could it
move?

As no answers were forthcoming, he took it that his guesses
were as good as his tormentors'. He took a single step forward
and paused again. Silence. He took another. Yes, the thing was
definitely glowing. It was what Pol would be after and apparently
would not have time to reach. Why not? Those approaching ships
of Mark's . . . ? Probably. So where would that leave him,
Mouseglove, even if he succeeded in making off with the bauble?
Had the Seven something more in mind for him? Or would he
finally be totally free, to go his own way?

Another step . . . Nothing. Two more quick ones . . .

A rustling, as of scales against stone . . .

He controlled a shudder and stepped again, over a small heap
of rubble. The rustling continued, as if something large and coiled
were unwinding itself.

*The grenade! Heave one down the well! Fall flat! Cover your
head!*

He did as he was told. The grenade was in his hand, then in the
air. As he threw himself forward behind the pedestal, he caught a
glimpse of an enormous, bright, feather-crowned head rising
above the low wall, of huge unblinking eyes, dark as pits, turned
in his direction, a green excrescence, like a blazing emerald, set in
the brow above them. Then an explosion shook the building.

A large block fell from the ceiling at the corner to the left of
the stair, followed by a fall of gravel and dirt, dust particles dancing in the light rays. The orange basket tumbled from its rest, the
rod rolling from it. It struck the lower step of the small pyramid,
bounced and came to rest beside Mouseglove's elbow.

You've got it! Take it and run!

He looked about, discovered it, seized it, scrambled to his feet.

Too late! he replied, the rod in his left hand, the blade in his
right. *It's not dead!*

An explosive hissing drowned the final rattlings of the stonefall.
The orange, red and pink-bonnetted head was swaying as if

disoriented, but moving steadily in his direction, too rapidly for him to escape it.

Strike at the jewel between the eyes!

He darted backward, raising the blade, knowing he would have but one chance.

As the serpent struck, so did he.

* * *

They burst into the dawn, retching and gasping, ears ringing, pulses pounding. Pol leaned forward and looked down at beaches running back to a line of lush tropical growth.

Down, Moonbird! We can barely hang on!

Moonbird dropped lower, slowing.

On the beach?

Yes. I want to bathe, to eat, to walk.

"Pol, I can't—"

"I know. Neither can I. Just another minute."

Moonbird settled gently. They slid off and lay unmoving on the sand. After a time, Pol reached out and touched Nora's hair.

"You did well," he said.

"You hung right in there, too." She patted Moonbird. "Good show." Then, "Where are we?" she asked.

How much farther?

We will reach it before the sun stands in the high places.

Good.

"We'll be there by noon," he said to Nora.

After a time, they undressed and bathed in the ocean, then cleaned their garments while Moonbird hunted and ate things that squealed a lot back among the trees. Their own breakfast was more silent as they watched the sun-dappled waves and fire-splashed clouds.

"I would like to sleep for an awfully long time," she finally said.

"We have been rather busy."

"When this is over, what are you going to do?"

"If I live," he said, "I would like to read the rest of the books in my father's library."

"And with that knowledge—what?"

"I look upon it as an end, not a means. I don't know what I'll do then. Oh, I want to rebuild Rondoval, of course, whether I stay or move on."

"Move on? To where?"

"I don't know. But I once traveled a golden road that went by wondrous places. Perhaps one day I'll walk it further and see more things."

"And will you be coming back if you do?"

"I think I must. Your land seems more like home to me than any other place I've ever lived."

"It's nice to have such choices," she said.

"If I live," he said.

When Moonbird returned, they stretched, brushed off sand and mounted, holding hands. The sun was higher and the jungle seemed greener now. They rose again, and soon Moonbird was bearing them south.

It was nearly noon when they sighted the stepped pyramid, approached it and began to circle.

You may be too late, Moonbird stated.

What do you mean?

Among the trees there are ships like the one you broke on the island.

I don't see . . .

I see their heat.

How many are there?

I count six.

I wonder how long they have been here? It could be an ambush.

Perhaps. What should I do?

I have to have that piece—

An explosion shook the pyramid.

"What—?" Nora began.

Go low and pass it fast. I want a better look.

Moonbird circled, positioned himself and began to fall. Pol

studied the jungle, still unable to detect the vessels of which the
dragon had spoken. As they descended, he turned his eyes toward
the pyramid itself. Clumps of dirt slid down its sides, and a minor
cave-in had occurred at one point. A cloud of dust rose like
smoke above the structure.

They passed through the dust and swept in low, regarding the
pyramid and the trees beyond it. Nothing stirred. Moonbird commenced climbing once again.

"Gods!" Nora shouted above the wind. "What is it?"

A small man in dark garments had just emerged, running, from
an opening in the far side of the pyramid. Moments later, a gigantic feathered head followed him out, to rise, swaying, tongue
flashing like fire or blood. It continued to emerge, at great length,
with such rapidity that the likelihood seemed strong that it would
soon fall upon the man.

*Moonbird! Stop! Go back! The jade strand— That man has the
rod!*

Moonbird was already braking, turning, growing warmer.

*It is the serpent of the well! I have always wanted to meet him
. . . You must slide off and run as soon as I strike. Take those
things you would preserve.*

Strike? No! You can't!

*I must! I have waited ages for this! It is also the only way to
save the man with your thing of power.*

Pol struck him with his fists, but it seemed unlikely that Moonbird even felt the blows.

"Get ready to jump down and run!" he cried to Nora, slinging
his guitar case, grabbing at the basket of water bottles.

The serpent heard the shout and turned its head upward.
Moonbird landed upon its back a moment later. Pol slipped off to
the right and began running. A great roaring and a loud hissing
rose up behind him. He felt a wave of heat. He saw the giant serpent body twisting toward him. He dodged it, looking about for
Nora as he moved. She was nowhere in sight. But the small man
with the rod had stumbled and picked himself up again. They
sighted one another at the same time, and Pol realized that it was
Mouseglove.

"Nora!" he shouted. "Can you see her?"

Mouseglove gestured toward the trees on the other side of the scaly turmoil. Nora had apparently jumped or been thrown in the opposite direction from Pol. He began circling, running toward Mouseglove, well past the place where Moonbird, caught in a colorful coil, had begun to spew smoldering liquids upon his twisting adversary. Ignition followed, and he smelled burning feathers as he ran. At about the same moment, he caught sight of Nora, surrounded by a large body of short, stocky men resembling those he had seen upon Anvil Mountain. Several of them lay unmoving among the grasses and Nora's left shoulder was bloodied. He saw there were dark cords wrapped around her, and that she was being pushed off among the trees.

At that moment, the reptilian combatants rolled toward them and they fled.

They came together among the high growth to the east, gasping, leaning upon vine and fungus-decked trees.

"Hurry!" Pol said, extending his hand. "The rod! I need it!"

Mouseglove passed it to him, a thin, long section, sculpted with clouds, the moon, stars and a celestial palace set above them, angelic spirits passing through the high places. Pol dropped it twice before he succeeded in fitting it into place at the end of the other sections. The feeling of power that washed over him as he did so was immense. It steadied his hands as it made his head swirl. He straightened.

"We have to go after her," he said, facing back toward the sounds of crashing and roaring. He pointed to the left of that place. "We can move faster if we return to the clearing, stay away from the fight, skirt the jungle."

Mouseglove nodded and put up his hand.

"I don't think we'll succeed, but I believe that she is safe for now, anyway."

"What do you mean?"

"I know those dwarves fairly well. She'd be dead by now if they didn't have orders not to kill her. They came here in flying ships and they'll doubtless take her back in one. They must be to them by now."

"I thought it was me they were after—or the last piece of this rod."

"Yes, but they'll avoid you rather than confront you now that you've got it. She was probably second choice—as hostage, possibly."

"What do you mean 'possibly'?"

"Mark likes her himself, you know."

"Yes, I know," Pol said. "Fill me in later. Let's move."

He raised the rod, and a blinding flash of white light leaped from it, cutting a path through the jungle. Without pausing, he headed forward along it.

When they came into the clearing once again, they saw that Moonbird and the feathered serpent were locked together, unmoving, pressed up against the side of the pyramid. The dragon was still caught within a coil, and his teeth were now locked upon the great snake's side. The serpent had his fangs fixed in Moonbird's left shoulder. A portion of the pyramid had collapsed about them.

As they turned and began to pass to their left, a sudden resumption of activity shook the ground. The singed serpent was thrown flat as Moonbird, wings freed, rose into the air, his shoulder still in the grip of his dangling adversary. Pol swung about and raised the rod.

No! The word vibrated along a green strand which suddenly sprang up between Moonbird and himself. *This is between us! Stay away!*

Without pausing to acknowledge the message, Pol continued on his way toward the place where Nora had been borne into the jungle, Mouseglove close behind him. There came another roar. Shortly, he smelled the stench of burning flesh. He did not look back.

They reached the spot where the bodies lay among the reddened grasses, Nora's blade protruding from one of them. Now that they were away from the scuffling beasts, other noises came to their ears—mechanical humming sounds from beyond the trees.

A dark shape rose into the air some distance to the south of them. Almost immediately, two more followed it.

"No!" Pol cried, and he raised the rod.

Mouseglove caught at his arm, dragging it down.

"You'll kill her if you shoot it down!" he shouted. "Besides, you've no way of knowing which one she's in. You can't afford to hit any of them!"

Pol's shoulders sagged. Two more vessels climbed into the air.

"Of course," he said, his arm falling. "Of course . . ."

He turned and looked at Mouseglove.

"Thanks," he said. Then, "I've got to go after her. I have to do what Mark wants—take things to a full conflict. He doesn't know what I've got to bring up against him, but he has to find out before he can embark on his campaign. Now he is about to learn. I'm going back there and take Anvil Mountain apart, if Moonbird can still fly . . ."

"I've got a ship," Mouseglove said. "I stole Mark's. I can fly it. I'll show you."

He took Pol's arm.

As they passed the pyramid again, the struggle was still in progress, with neither combatant showing any sign of weakening. Great furrows and pits had been torn in the charred ground; thick, sweet-smelling blood was smeared everywhere, and both dragon and serpent were soaked in it. At the moment, they were so intertwined that it was impossible for Pol to assess their damages, let alone to use the rod on Moonbird's behalf.

He summoned the strand by which Moonbird had addressed him earlier.

I must return to Rondoval now and prepare for battle, he said. *Mark has Nora. Mouseglove can take me there in his flier. I cannot await the outcome of your struggle.*

Go. When it is finished, I will return.

Immediately, the two began to thrash about again. The serpent, half of its feathers missing, began to hiss violently. Flames blossomed about it, upon it, as Pol and Mouseglove hurried by. It succeeded just then in throwing a coil about Moonbird's neck, but the dragon's claws were now raking its midsection.

"Tell him to go for the green jewel in the thing's head," Mouseglove said. "I stunned it for a moment when I hit it there."

Strike at the jewel in its head, Pol immediately relayed to Moonbird, but there was no reply.

They hurried past, coming shortly to the trail Mouseglove had hacked through the brush.

"This way," said the smaller man. "I've concealed it in a place not too far ahead. But—Pol, I'm too tired to make the flight all the way back. I'd fall asleep and kill us both."

"Just get us airborne," Pol replied. "I'll watch and ask questions. We can take turns flying, if necessary."

"You look fairly tired yourself."

"I am. But it is not going to be as long a haul as you might think."

They entered a cleared area. Mouseglove paused and gestured, crossed to a green mound, began removing fronds.

"What do you mean?" he asked. "I just made the trip."

Pol moved to assist him.

"You're not going to like it," he said, "but I know a short-cut . . ."

XIX.

. . . He strode past the glassed-in banks of flat-faced machines, their huge metal eyes rotating, stopping, reversing, rotating again, ceaselessly, silently, to his left. To his right, a line of men and women, seated before glowing screens, traced designs with electric pencils upon them. The rug was soft and resilient, making the floor seem almost nonexistent. A gentle light emanated from glowing tubes overhead. The abstract design upon the wall to the right changed as he passed. A soft, characterless music filled the air . . .

. . . He halted when he came to the large window looking out upon the city. Far below, numerous vehicles passed on the streets. Boats moved upon the distant river, and an airplane was passing overhead. Towering buildings dominated the prospect, and everything was clean and shining and smooth, like a piece of well-tended machinery. A certain warmth grew in his breast as he regarded the power and magnificence of the scene. His fingers tapped at a latch, and he drew the window upward, leaning forward to drink in the full range of sensations which emanated from the city . . .

. . . A heavy hand fell upon his shoulder, and he turned toward the tall, heavyset man who stood smiling beside him, drink in hand, face as ruddy as brick, red hair mingled with white, red scalp showing through . . .

". . . Yes, Mark, admire it," he was saying, gesturing with his glass. "One day, all of that will be yours . . ."

. . . He turned to look again, having drawn back slightly from the aura of power which surrounded the larger man. Something at the left side of his face clicked against the window's frame. Raising his hand to explore, he discovered a huge protruberance above his left eye. Immediately, he remembered that it had been there all along. Turning farther, with something like shame, he reached up and touched it again . . .

. . . His vision doubled. Beyond the window now, he saw two discrete scenes. Half of the city before him was still bright and beckoning. The other half was gray, drab, the air filled with ashes and yellowish fog-like tentacles. Raucous noises, as of the rattling of heavy machinery rose up on that side of the split scene, accompanied by a wave of acrid odors. Moist, sickly patches of color clung to the buildings. The river was muddy. The ships' smokestacks poured filth into the air . . .

. . . He drew back, turning again toward the big man, to discover that he, also, had doubled. The man to the right stood unchanged; the one on the left was even redder, his face partly shadowed, eyes flashing baleful lights . . .

". . . What is the matter, my son?" he was asking.

. . . Mark could not speak. He gestured toward the window, turning slightly in that direction, to discover that the scene was no longer split. The left side had superimposed itself upon his entire field of vision. His father merged also at that moment, and only the darker version remained . . .

. . . Gesturing frantically, Mark tried to inform him as to what had occurred. Suddenly, a dragon appeared above the skyline, Pol mounted upon its back, headed in their direction . . .

". . . Oh, him," the shadowy figure at his side was saying. "He is a troublemaker. I cast him out long ago. He comes seeking to destroy you. Be strong . . ."

. . . Mark stared as the figure grew larger and larger, until finally it was crashing, soundlessly, through the wall, reaching for him. Then there came a knocking sound, growing louder as it was repeated. Everything began to come apart about him, and he was falling . . .

He sat up in his bed, drenched with perspiration. The knocking continued. He rose and turned on the light, despite the fact that his left eye saw clearly. Throwing his robe about his shoulders, he moved to the door and opened it. The small man drew back, extending a piece of paper. "You asked to see this as soon as it came in, sir."

He glanced at it and lowered it.

"We have Nora, and Pol got away with the magical device," he stated.

"Yes, sir. They're already in the air, bringing her here."

"Good. Notify the force at Rondoval that he may be on his way back there." He looked out, past his new flier, into the night. "I'd better check on the status of our mobilization. Return to duty."

"Yes, sir."

When he had finished dressing, he withdrew the photograph from his night table and stared at it for a time.

"We'll see," he said, "who falls."

* * *

Mouseglove was at the controls as they neared Rondoval.

"I don't see how you can seem so rested," he remarked, "after such a short nap. Mine didn't do me that much good—not after that damned shortcut of yours."

He looked about the messy cabin and wrinkled his nose.

"I seem to be drawing some sort of energy from the scepter," Pol answered. "It feels as though I have an extra heart or lung, or both. That—"

A puff of smoke appeared above the battlements.

"What was that?" Mouseglove asked, as two more appeared.

"It almost seems as if it could be gunfire. Veer off. I don't want to take—" The ship shuddered, as if from a heavy blow. "—any

chances," Pol finished, bracing himself and seizing the rod with his right hand.

A moment later they were falling, smoke coming into the cabin.

"Is it out of control?" Pol shouted.

"Not completely," Mouseglove replied, "but I can't pull it up. I'm trying to miss the rocks, at least. Maybe those trees over there . . . Can you do anything?"

"I don't know."

Pol raised the scepter and strands were drawn to it through all the walls. To his eyes, it seemed again as if he sat at the center of an enormous, three-dimensional spiderweb. All of the strands began pulsing in time with the throbbing that rose in his wrist. The ship seemed to slow.

"We're going to miss the rocks!" Mouseglove shouted.

Perspiration sprang forth on Pol's brow. The lines between his eyes deepened.

"We're going to crash!"

A final burst of power fled from the scepter along the strands. Then there were treetops before them, upthrust branches reaching, then breaking. Abruptly, they came up against one which did not yield and they were pitched forward at the impact. The ship was torn open about them, but they were not aware of it.

Pol came awake with his hands tied behind him and did not open his eyes, as all his recent memories were immediately present within his throbbing head. He heard voices and smelled horses. There followed a sound of retreating hoofbeats. If whoever had shot at them had ridden down from the castle, the fact that they had not killed him immediately seemed to offer some sort of chance. He tested his bonds and found them very secure. He wondered how long he had been unconscious, and he wondered whether Mouseglove had survived the crash. And the scepter . . . Where was it?

He opened his eyes to the barest of slits and began turning his head, slowly.

He flinched, just slightly. But that was sufficient. He had not expected to see a centaur.

"Aha! You are awake!" cried the horse-man, who had apparently been scrutinizing him.

The well-muscled human torso towered above the sorrel horse-body, long black hair pulled back from the dark-eyed, heavy-featured, masculine face and tied behind the head in something, Pol almost giggled, that he had once known as a pony tail.

"I am awake," he acknowledged, heaving himself toward a sitting position.

He succeeded on the second try. He saw Mouseglove lying on his side, hands similarly bound, still apparently unconscious, perhaps four meters away, beneath a large tree. The guitar case, apparently unscathed, rested against the tree's trunk. Pieces of wreckage lay between them, and when he looked upward, he saw the balance of the flier hanging like a giant, squashed fruit among the branches.

"Why have you tied us up?" he asked. "We've done nothing to you."

"Ha!" snorted his captor, executing a small prancing maneuver. "You call murder nothing?"

"In this case, yes," Pol replied, "since I've no idea what you are talking about."

The centaur stepped nearer, as if considering abusing him. Behind him, Pol saw Mouseglove stir. There seemed to be no other centaurs about, though the ground bore a great number of hoofmarks.

"Is it not possible that you could be mistaken?" Pol continued. "I know of no deaths hereabout—unless a piece of our ship fell on someone—"

"Liar," said the centaur, leaning forward and glaring directly into his eyes. "You came in your ships and slaughtered my people." He gestured toward the wreckage in the treetop. "You even kidnapped one of them. You deny this?"

The hoofs were darting and dancing uncomfortably near him as Pol shook his head.

"I do," he said, staring back, "but I would like to know more about what happened, if I'm to be blamed for it."

The centaur wheeled and paced away from him, kicking dust

into his face. Pol shook his head, which had begun aching more severely, and he automatically called for healing strands to wrap it, as he had for his neck wound. They came and attached themselves to his brow, draining away some of the pain. He thought of his wrist then, but it was partly numbed by the pressure of the cord. He wondered whether he could manipulate strands in more complicated patterns without seeing what he was about, or whether there might be some other way to gain control over his captor.

"The others have gone to fetch a warrior to decide what to do with you," the centaur stated. "She may wish to talk about these things. I don't. It should not be long, though. I believe that I hear them approaching now."

Pol listened but heard nothing. A purple strand settled near him, its farther end passing across the centaur's shoulder. He willed that it come into contact with his fingertips. It passed behind him, and shortly he felt a tingling in his left hand. His fingers twisted. There came a familiar sensation of power.

"Look at me," he said.

The centaur turned.

"What do you want?"

Pol caught his gaze with his own. From his left hand, he felt the power move.

"You are so tired that you are almost asleep on your feet," he said. "Now you are, but don't bother closing your eyes. You can hear only my voice."

The centaur's gaze grew distant. His breathing slowed. He began to sway.

". . . But you can move about just as if you were awake, when I tell you to. My hands have been tied by mistake. Come over here and free them."

He rose to his feet and turned. The centaur came up behind him and began fumbling at the knots. Pol recalled seeing a knife at the creature's side.

"Cut the bonds," he ordered. "Quickly!"

A moment later, he was rubbing his wrists.

"Give me the knife."

He accepted the blade, crossed to where Mouseglove lay beneath the tree, watching him.

"Are you hurt?" he asked, as he faced the smaller man.

"I ache all over. But then, I felt that way before the crash, too. I don't believe anything is broken."

Mouseglove stood and turned about, raising his hands. As Pol slit the cord, he said, "Must be Mark's people in your castle. No one else has weapons like that— Uh-oh."

The sound of hoofbeats now came to their ears.

"Shall we run for it?" Mouseglove asked.

"No. Too late. They'd catch us. We'll wait and have this out here."

Pol slipped the knife behind his belt and turned to face the wood. A mental order to the centaur he now controlled moved him off to the right.

Shortly, the figures came into sight—four male centaurs led by an older female. She halted, about ten meters from where he stood, and regarded Pol.

"I was told you were bound," she stated.

"I was."

She stepped forward, and Pol started as he saw that she held the scepter in the hand which had been out of sight at her side. She raised it and pointed it at him. He saw a cluster of strands rush toward it. He issued a mental command and the centaur under his spell stepped between them. New spells suggested themselves to him and he summoned strands of his own.

The female centaur's eyes widened.

"What have you done to him?" she asked.

"Return my rod and we'll talk about it."

From the corner of his eye, Pol saw that Mouseglove was edging away.

"Where did you get it?" she asked.

"I recovered it, piece by piece, from the points of the Triangle of Int."

"Only a sorcerer could do that."

"You noticed."

"I, too, have some familiarity with the Art, though only the middle part of this rod will respond to me. Mine is an Earth magic." She gestured upward. "Why then were you riding in that thing?"

"My dragon was occupied. That vessel was stolen from my enemy, Mark Marakson, who has many such, atop Anvil Mountain. Perhaps you have seen his dark birds, who are not of flesh, in the skies."

"I know who he is and I have seen such birds. Some of my people were killed and some injured by men who came in larger vessels such as the one you rode."

The strands came into his hands and Pol felt the power throb in his wrist. Still, he had no wish to face a person who could use even the middle section of the rod.

"Small men, I daresay," he answered, "for such is the stature of the race which serves him. I have never harmed a centaur and I've no desire to. This will be the first time, if you force me to fight here."

"Sunfa, come forward," she said, and a smaller male moved from among those to the rear of the group to a position beside her. There was a long gash upon his left shoulder, and he was missing several teeth. "Were either of these men of the party which attacked you that day?"

He shook his head.

"No, Stel. Neither of them."

Her head snapped forward.

"You know my name now," she said. "So know, too, that I was among the force which stormed Rondoval the day this rod was wrested from Det Morson."

Pol raised his right hand so that his sleeve fell back, revealing the dragonmark.

"I am Pol Detson," he stated. "I have heard stories concerning my father. But I was taken from this land as a child and raised in another place. I never knew him. The past is dead, so far as I am concerned. I have only been back for a short while. I need that scepter for purposes of arousing the forces of Rondoval against those of Anvil Mountain. Are you going to return it to me?"

"In many ways," she replied, "this is even more disturbing than your being what we had thought you. For the moment, it is good if our enemy is also your enemy. But to see the hordes that lie beneath Rondoval roused once again is a frightening thought, especially for those of us who were alive in your father's day. So tell me, what do you propose doing when your battle is over?"

Pol laughed.

"You are assuming that I win and that I live. But, all right . . . I would lay most of my forces to rest again. I would like to be left alone to pursue my studies, and I would be happy to return the favor and leave everyone else in the neighborhood to his own devices. After a time, I may do some traveling. I don't know. I am not attracted by the darker aspects of the Art. I have no desire to conquer anything, and the idea of ruling over anybody bores the ass off me."

"Commendable," she said, "and I find myself wanting to believe you. In fact, it seems likely that you are telling the truth. However, even granting that, people do change. I would like very much to see you deal with the people who feel that they can hunt centaurs whenever they choose. But I would also like some assurance that you will not one day be inclined to do it yourself."

"My word is all that I can give you. Take it or leave it."

"But you could give me more—and in return, your own way might be eased."

"What have you in mind?"

"Swear an oath of friendship with us, upon your scepter."

"Friendship is a thing that goes further than nonaggression," he replied. "It is something that works both ways."

"I will be willing to swear the same oath for you."

"On your own, or on behalf of the other centaurs as well?"

"For all of us."

"You can speak for them?"

"I can."

"Very well. I'll do it if you will."

He looked back at Mouseglove, who was about to slip off among the trees.

"Stay put," he called back. "You're safe."

"For now," Mouseglove replied. But he returned.

Pol moved around the cataleptic centaur who stood between Stel and himself, destroying the spell which held him with a twisting motion of his hand as he passed. That one drew away, eyes shifting rapidly, until Stel spoke some reassurance.

"Tell me the words of the oath," Pol said, coming up before her.

"Place your hand upon the middle section of the rod, and repeat after me."

Pol nodded and complied.

As she began to speak the words, a series of dark strands knotted themselves about them. He felt a vaguely threatening force accumulating within them. When they had finished speaking, the knots separated and drifted away, like small, dark clouds. One went to hover behind Stel. He felt such a presence behind himself, also.

"There," she said, passing the rod to him. "We have created our own dooms, should we betray one another."

They clasped hands.

"No problem then," Pol answered, smiling, "and it's good to have some friends. I'd like to stay and visit, but now I've some monsters to rouse. Hopefully, I'll be back."

He turned away and fetched his guitar case.

"A weapon?" she asked as he raised it.

"No, a musical instrument. Maybe I'll be able to play it for you one day."

"You are really going to Rondoval now?"

"I must."

"Give me time to raise a force, to rid the place of your enemies. Now we are allies, it is our fight, too."

"Not necessary," Pol said. "They are up in the castle. My destination is far below it. Moonbird—my dragon—showed me a tunnel to the place. I'll go in that way and bypass the bastards. There is no need at all to deal with them now."

"Where does the tunnel open?"

"Down the slope, to the north. I'll have to do a little climbing, but I foresee no real difficulties."

"—Unless your enemies see you and go after you in their flying boats."

He shrugged.

"There is always that chance."

"So I will take a small force and lead a diversionary assault from the south. Two of my males will bear you and your friend to the northern slope."

"The enemy has guns, which kill from a distance."

"So do arrows. We'll take no unnecessary risks. I am going to send runners now, to tell the others to arm and to bring them here. While we wait, I would like to hear your music."

"Okay. Me, too," said Pol. "Let's get comfortable."

XX.

"You were with him," Mark said to Nora, as they both leaned upon the railing to his roof garden. "What is his power, anyway, now he has that scepter?"

"I don't know," she replied, looking at the flowers. "I really don't know. I'm not even sure that he was absolutely certain. Or else he was being very close-mouthed."

"Well, I think it possible that he is dead. On the other hand, I've no idea how he got across the ocean as quickly as he did. He has something going for him. He was in my flier at one point—and it was shot down near Rondoval. Still . . . Supposing—just supposing—he is still alive? How would he attack me? What sort of forces might he bring?"

She shook her head and looked at him. His lens was a pale blue and he was smiling.

"I couldn't tell you, Mark," she said, "and if I could . . ."

"You wouldn't? I'd guessed that much. It didn't take long, did it? For you to fall in love with a flashy traveler with a good story?"

"You really believe that, don't you?"

"What else am I to think? We've known each other most of our lives. I thought we had something of an understanding. Then, practically overnight, you're in love with a stranger."

"I am not in love with Pol," she said, straightening. "Oh, it could happen, very easily. He's quick and strong—clever, attractive. But, really I hardly know him, despite what we've been through together. On the other hand, I thought that I knew you—very well—and now I see that I was mistaken about a great number of things. If you want honesty, rather than sweet words, I am not, at this moment, in love with anyone."

"But did you once feel that way about me?"

"I thought that I did."

He hammered his fist against the rail.

She laid a hand on his shoulder.

"It's this lens, isn't it? This damned, ugly bug-eye!"

"Don't be silly," she said. "I wasn't talking about appearance. I

was talking about what you are doing. You've always been different. You've always had a way with mechanical things. That in itself is hardly bad, but what you are doing—what you are planning to do—with your knowledge and your contrivances—that is."

"Don't let's go into it again."

She withdrew her hand.

"You asked me. If he still lives, Pol has to fight you—some way—now. Sometimes it almost seems that a conflict between the two of you was ordained before you both were born. Other times

I've thought of it, though, it seemed that it need not be so. You could be friends. He is the closest thing you have to a relative. And it is probably that way for him, also. I will tell you what I told him. I feel like a pawn. You are jealous of him, and he will want to rescue me from you. I almost feel as if my life has been somehow manipulated to bring me into this position, to insure that a battle will occur. I wish that I'd never met either of you!"

She turned away. He guessed that she was crying, but was not certain. He began to extend his hand.

"Sir! Sir!"

A captain of his guard was rushing toward him. Scowling, Mark turned.

"What is it?"

"Castle Rondoval is under attack! The message just came through! Should we send reinforcements?"

"Who is attacking? How? What are the details?"

"There are none. The message was short, garbled. We are waiting for an answer."

"Divert all the nearest birds. Get me a picture of what's going on. I'll be down there shortly. We're going on alert."

He raised his hand and two guards, pretending to study the garden from its opposite end, immediately moved toward him.

"I'd wager your lover lives," he said, "and that this is his doing. At any rate, your talk of pawns has given me an idea. Guards! Take her away. Protect her. Watch her well. She may be of some use yet."

Turning on his heel, he headed toward the elevator. He did not look back.

*　*　*

Mouseglove moved with near-acrobatic skill up the final few meters of the cliff-face, hauled himself into the cavemouth, turned, stooped and assisted Pol.

"All right," he said then, "I am about to keep a promise. I vowed that if they would leave me alone, I would bring them back to Rondoval." He groped beneath his cloak and withdrew a parcel. "They did and I have. So here."

He handed the package to Pol.

"I don't understand. What is it?" Pol asked.

"The figurines of the seven sorcerers I stole from your father. As you gained sections of that scepter, they grew in power until finally they were able to control me. During the trip back here, I told you everything I had done, but I didn't tell you why. They are the reason. Surely, you don't think I'd go and play games with a feathered serpent for laughs? They are powerful, they can communicate if they want—and I have no idea what they are up to. Also, they are all yours now. Don't worry, though. A big part of their purpose in life seems to be taking care of you. I would try to learn more about them soon, if I were you."

"I wish I had time," Pol remarked, "but I don't. Not now." He secured the parcel at his belt and turned. The dragon-light sprang forth to dart before them. "Let's go."

Mouseglove fell into step beside him.

"I wonder how the centaurs are doing?" he said.

Pol shrugged.

"I hope they get the message soon that we made it safely. If the two who brought us hurry, they will. Then they can lay off and return to the woods."

"If you really meant that oath, perhaps you ought to send something particularly nasty upstairs to clear the halls."

"Why?"

"I've seen how centaurs fight. They're tough, but they also get kind of frenzied after awhile. I've a hunch they won't be falling back."

"Really? I didn't know that."

"Oh, yes. So, surely you could spare a dragon or an ogre or two, to clean house and protect your new friends."

"I guess I should."

They walked on for a time, following the pale light. At several points they had to climb down over rocky irregularities.

"Uh, I guess we'll be parting company soon," Mouseglove said as they entered the first of a series of larger caverns. "I've done what I came back to do, and I promised myself I'd never set foot on Anvil Mountain again."

"I didn't expect you to accompany me there," Pol replied, "and it's not your fight. What have you in mind to do now?"

"Well, after your servant's made it safe for the likes of me upstairs, I'll head in that direction. Be sure to tell him that I'm okay. I'll borrow some fresh garments, if that's all right with you, clean up, have a nap and be moving on."

They passed a large, winged, sleeping form.

"You have my permission, my thanks and my blessing," Pol said. "Also my ogre, to clear your way."

Mouseglove chuckled.

"You are a difficult young man to gull. I'm actually coming to like you. Pity, we'll probably never meet again."

"Who knows? I'll ask the Seven when I get a chance."

"I'd rather you didn't remind them of me."

The next cavern they entered was even larger, though more level. Pol looked at the humped and massed bodies among which they made their way. There seemed to be no way of estimating their number, though the strands ran thick and numerous through the gloom.

As they trudged on, coming at last into the major cavern and starting across it, Pol finally glimpsed the soft glow of the master spell at its farther end.

"Tell me," he asked, "do you see any light in that direction?"

"No. Just the one we're following."

Pol gestured and seized a strand. Soon it took on a pale color and something of incandescence.

"See that?"

"A line of light, running before us."

"Good. I'll give you one of that sort to follow out. What is that thing in your hand?"

"A pistol I've carried since I left Mark's place."

"I thought so. You won't need it here."

"It comforts me."

After a considerable interval, they stood before the pied globe. Pol held the scepter as he faced it.

"I hope this works as I'd anticipated," he remarked.

"I feel some force, but I see nothing special . . ."

"Go and stand over in that niche." He gestured, and for a moment the scepter blazed like a captive star. "I will tell you when it is safe to depart. There is your strand." He gestured again, and a line of pale fire grew in the air before the niche. "Good luck!"

"To you, also," Mouseglove replied, clasping Pol's hand and turning.

He moved quickly and backed into the opening, unable to take his eyes from the spectacle of the younger man, who had already begun a series of seeming ritual movements, his silhouette distorted by guitar case and flapping cloak, his face pale and masklike in the blaze of the rod, beneath the dark, silver-splashed wings of his hair. Mouseglove clutched the pistol more tightly as the slow dance of the hand and the rod progressed, for he felt a chill followed by a wave of warmth, another chill . . . and now he had momentary flashes of vision, as of a massive, burning ball of yarn being unwound.

Pol moved his hand deftly, in and out, unwinding, unravelling, and old words trapped within the fabric of the structure, came to him and he spoke them as he worked, and the waves of heat came more frequently, till finally he saw through to the center, the core, the end . . .

He thrust the scepter into the heart of the spell and spoke the final words.

A great wash of forces swept by him and he swayed, striving to keep his balance. The strands now clung to the scepter, obscuring it completely to Pol's vision. His right arm seemed to take fire as he laid his will upon it.

A moaning rose within the cavern, growing to a mighty chorus of sounds, which echoed and reechoed about him, followed by rustling, scraping noises and the falling of stones.

". . . Arise! Arise! and follow me to battle!" he sang, and now there were larger movements within the darkness.

The moaning died down and ceased. The snorts, snarls, roars and rattles diminished. Now the sounds of heavy breathing came to him from every direction.

He plucked a single strand, and soon a huge, gray form moved past him on two legs, hunched forward, arms dragging on the ground, yellow eyes burning within the darkness of a triangular face, scales rustling with each stride. It paused before Mouseglove, who raised the pistol and waited, but it turned and moved on an instant later.

"Give it an hour." Pol stated, "and the upstairs should be cleared. It knows you now and will not harm you."

Mouseglove nodded, realizing as he did that the movement could not be seen, but unable to control his voice. Brief bonfires flared and died at all distances as dragons tested their flames.

Pol turned away, directing all his attention to impressing his identity and his commands upon the awakening creatures.

Arise, I say! We fly south to destroy the city atop Anvil Mountain! Those of you who cannot fly must be mounted upon those who can! I will lead the way!

He cast about for only a moment, and then his fingers moved unerringly to catch at a dark green strand drifting near him.

Dragon! he called. *Name yourself!*

I am called Smoke-in-the-Skies-at-Evening-against-the-Last-Pale-Clouds-of-Autumn-Day, came a proud feminine reply.

In the interest of ready communication, I shall refer to you as 'Smoke.'

That is agreeable to me.

Come to me now. We must lead the others.

For a time, nothing occurred, as he realized that Smoke had slept within one of the farther caverns. All of the stirring sounds grew louder as the other creatures stood, stretched, mounted. Finally, he heard a noise like a rising wind rushing toward him, and a piece of darkness detached itself from the distant shadows, to sweep in his direction and settle silently before him.

Greetings, Pol Detson. I am ready, she said.

He released the strand and moved to touch her neck.

Greetings, Smoke. If I may mount now, we will be on our way.

Come up. I am ready.

Pol climbed toward her shoulders and settled into position. He raised the scepter and lights danced throughout the cavern.

Follow! he ordered. Then, to Smoke, *Now! Let us go!*

Smoke was smaller than Moonbird but seemed faster. In a matter of moments, they were airborne and moving ahead quickly. Pol looked back once. He could not distinguish Mouseglove in his niche, but he saw that dark forms were rising like ashes in his wake.

You will sing us a battle-song? Smoke asked.

Pol was surprised to find it already upon his lips.

XXI.

The bird-things sent to determine the nature and progress of the conflict at Rondoval were the first observers of the dragon-flight which began at the northern cliff-face below the castle, spiraling upward, wheeling through the west and falling into a sky-darkening pattern heading southward, led by a man mounted upon a sleek gray dragon, a shining scepter in his right hand. The sun settled as they flew, and the metallic birds climbed and moved far to the right and the left to monitor their progress.

Mark assigned troops to the various stations, and the elevators ground ceaselessly as tanks and artillery pieces were raised from the warehouse areas to the streets of the city proper. Weapons and ammunition were issued to the defenders. All available sky boats were serviced and armed. Assembly lines were shut down, and the workers went to collect their weapons.

Mark studied the array of screens in the surveillance center, showing varied views of the oncoming formation.

"I'd like to know what those things can do," he remarked to the captain who stood at his elbow. "This could be closer than I'd care to see it. Who'd have thought he could raise something like that this quickly? Damned sorcerer! Send a dozen battle-wagons to hit them at dawn. Swing six of them wide to hit their left flank out of the sunrise, and drop six on them from above. We'll probably lose them, but I want to see how it happens."

"Yes, sir."

Mark toyed with the idea of sending for Nora, but dismissed it. He visited the lab instead, to check whether a long-range jumble was yet possible. He doubted it, but something useful might yet be salvaged from that project.

. . . Damn! he mused. A year from now and he'd never make it across the desert. I know about more things than I've got. Can't get them into production fast enough . . . Damn!

His lens was a pale yellow beneath a perfectly clear sky. Stars winked at him and a warm breeze licked like an affectionate tiger at his cheek. Suddenly, a meteor shower began, and he watched it for several minutes, dismissing the shaking beneath his feet as the labors of the heavy machinery which had long since been shut down.

*   *   *

Pol fled across the night, the power of the scepter his meat, his drink and his sleep. When the attack came in the morning, he spread the formation, detached two groups of ten dragons each to deal with the sky boats and continued on. Later, sixteen dragons rejoined him, but two of them had to drop out, their injuries preventing them from maintaining the pace of the others. He led the entire formation to a greater altitude after that and began spreading it into a great line. Through the morning hazes, the ground seemed to ripple momentarily beneath them.

He saw the advancing formation of flying things just before Anvil Mountain came into view.

Destroy as many as are necessary to get through, he ordered the leather-winged masses at his back. *But do not remain to toy with them. I doubt they will bomb or strafe once you are into their own city fighting with its defenders. Destroy anything on the mountain that offers resistance. Then burn the place. Only this girl*—and he sent a mental picture of Nora back along the strands —*must not be harmed. If you see her, protect her. And this one*—a picture of Mark followed—*is mine. Call to me if you see him.*

They swept on toward the line of defenders and shortly the firing began. A little while after that, dragon vomit fell like rain upon the sky boats. Fires dotted the ground, wreckage and falling bodies filled the air. There were a great many of the ships, but their crews could not reload the guns quickly and their accuracy was far less than perfect. After several minutes of combat, it was clear that Pol's forces would not be halted here. When they finally passed on toward Anvil Mountain, their force was diminished but the air fleet was broken.

As they came within range of the flat-topped mount, the artil-

lery fire began. But Pol had spread his formation even more thinly by then, having seen evidence of heavy artillery on his earlier visit to the place.

Still, the great guns fired with deadly effect for several minutes, until two of them toppled, one exploded and others began firing wildly.

Sweeping even nearer, through the morning light, Pol saw that the entire mountain was shaking.

It is a mighty magic you wield, Smoke remarked.

That is not my doing, he replied.

A dragon can feel magic, and that which leads to the earthquake I feel upon my back.

I do not understand.

The answer hangs at your belt.

The figurines?

I know not what they are, only what they are bringing to pass.

Good! I'll take all the help I can get!

Even if they control you?

Either way, I have no choice now but to try to win, do I?

They broke through the openings in the artillery screen, dragons landing and discharging the non-winged creatures which immediately turned and sought the defenders. Tanks rumbled along the shaking streets, some of them spewing flames back at the dragons.

A steady crackling of gunfire rose above the city. The metallic worms were out, wrestling with the attackers. Here and there, blades flashed in the hands of men as ammunition was exhausted. The howling, bounding lesser beasts of the caverns tore through the city, killing and being killed. A crack opened, diagonally, in one of the main avenues and noxious fumes rose out of it.

Pol looked about, searching rooftops and opened bunkers, hoping to catch sight of the red-haired man with the eye of many colors. But Mark was nowhere in sight.

He sought altitude again, and he directed Smoke to take him in a wide circle above the city. The screens grew fainter as they rose, and the designs of the buildings and the overall layout of the city impressed themselves upon him for the first time. The place was efficiently disposed, extremely functional, logically patterned and relatively clean. He realized that he felt a grudging admiration for a country boy capable of materializing such a dream—and in such a brief while—whether his world wanted it or not. He wished once again that he could have sent Mark back to the place where he himself had been so long the misfit.

They landed upon the vacant roof of a tall building; and there, without dismounting, Pol raised the scepter with both hands and laid his will upon his forces below. They required organization now, not skirmishing. It was time to create groups and direct their efforts toward specific objectives. His wrist pulsed, the rod pulsed, the strands pulsed as he began. There was usually a feeling of elation as he worked with the power. But this time, while the feeling was present, there was little joy accompanying it. He had never wished to be the destroyer of another man's dreams.

He saw tanks torn apart by his creatures, but he also saw dragons beset and hacked apart by the small folk, who, having moved from the wilds to this existence in the span of a few years, still possessed the instincts of pack hunters when reduced to the bloody basics of life. He felt something of an admiration for them, also, though this in no way affected his tactics. He grew more and more dispassionate as the sun climbed and the conflicts progressed. Moving each time artillery pieces were repositioned to bring him down, directing strike forces toward the most troublesome emplacements, he hurled other assaults against what appeared to be nerve centers, breaking down walls and spreading fires, wondering the while whether Mark occupied some similar position elsewhere, and with radio communication directed his forces into the surprising patterns of resistance which kept developing. Most likely. Things were still too closely balanced to permit him to desert his command post and seek the other out, however. The casualties were heavy on both sides. Pol felt he now had the edge, though, in that he was destroying more and more of his adversary's capabilities as the day progressed, whereas his own forces were not dependent upon things outside themselves. He was slowly reducing them to reliance upon the simplest of weapons, and when this reduction had reached the proper point, a parity of forces would represent no equality what-soever and the battle would be near to its end.

The mountain gave another shudder, and the opening in the ground grew larger. Steam had emerged from it for a long while, earlier, but with the enlargement flames and pieces of stone shot forth, the buildings nearby suffered partial collapse of their facades and a roaring noise came up, growing until it smothered all the sounds of the fighting.

Pol's aching hands tightened even more upon the scepter, as he said aloud, "Only a fool could call it coincidence. If I've an un-seen ally, make yourself known!"

Immediately, seven large flames hovered in the air before him, unsupported by any burning medium. The one to his left flick-ered, and the reply seemed to come from that source:

It is no coincidence.

"Why, then?"

Now the second flame flickered.

It is a recurring thing, this struggle. Ages ago, the world was split by it, giving birth to the one in which you were raised, where we are legend, and making that one a legend to this. It is an un-dying conflict and its time has come again. You are the agent of preservation; Mark, the champion of the insurgency. One of you must be utterly obliterated.

"Has he allies such as you?"

The third replied:

Beneath that shrine, far below, is an ancient teaching machine. He bears a small unit within his body which keeps him in con-stant communication with it.

Pol immediately disengaged a force and directed it against the shrine, with instructions to destroy everything beneath it as well.

"Do you already know the outcome here?" he asked.

It is still undecided, said the fourth.

We distract you, said the fifth.

. . . And your full attention is still required here, said the sixth.

. . . And so we depart, said the seventh, as they faded and dwindled to nothing.

Pol was immediately beset by a fresh artillery barrage, and had to fly to a new vantage while directing attacks against the guns.

Strong fumes reached him before very long, and he had to move again, seeing now that the opening below had become a glowing crater, its smoke rising to smudge the sky. Its rumbles continued to grow, also.

Much later, he realized that no one was shooting at him any longer. Suicide fliers had attacked for a time, but he had destroyed them with blasts from the scepter until, finally, they had ceased.

The fighting below had grown more and more disorganized, as both sides suffered massive casualties. The battle for the shrine, far down below the slopes, continued. A remarkably powerful defense had seemed to arise from almost nowhere, and Pol had diverted more forces to deal with it.

. . . And Nora thought herself a pawn, he reflected. *What am I? I exercise all the functions of command, yet I am no freer than any of those below. Unless . . .*

Up, Smoke! Big circles!

I, too, serve, came the reply, and they were rising, turning.

The third time around, he saw them—Nora and Mark atop a high building, across the avenue from the crater. It was a flash of sunlight gleaming upon a red lens turned in his direction that drew his eyes to their position.

Over there, Smoke! It still may not be too late to talk to him! If I can just make him see what is happening!

Smoke turned and beat toward the rooftop. Pol waved his dirty handkerchief, doubting that the gesture meant anything in this place, but willing to try anything he knew to gain conversation with the other.

"Mark!" he shouted. "I want to talk! May I come down?"

The other lowered a small unit into which he had been speaking and gestured for him to land.

As soon as Smoke touched the roof, Pol leaped down and headed toward the tall figure with the yellowing eye lens.

"I am only now beginning to realize what we are doing," Pol said, while he was still moving. "It was an encounter such as this, between science and magic, which destroyed a high culture in this land ages ago, which split the continuum into parallel parts. We are doing it again! We are both victims! We've been manipulated. This battle is affecting the land itself! We have to—"

An explosion at his back caused him to stumble forward. Whether the great cry from Smoke was mental or verbal, he never knew.

"Damn you, Mark!" he called as he got to his feet, not even looking back, already knowing what he would see. "I came here to save your life, to stop this thing—"

"How considerate," Mark stated. "In that case, I accept your surrender."

"Don't be an ass!" Pol staggered to the edge of the shuddering building. "Surrender what? Look down there! Both of our armies are almost finished. We can still stop it. Right here. We can still save something. Both science and magic do work here—so it is not an either/or proposition in this place. They must both be special cases of some more general law. Let's work out something compatible. Let's not go the way we're being pushed. If the continuum must be split again, let's split it our way. I'll work with you. But look down there! Look what's happening! Do you want that?"

Mark moved to the low, partly shattered parapet, followed by Nora. Pol saw that he held her wrist in a powerful grip. He looked down again himself, to where a fiery river now flowed along the avenue, away from the still growing crater almost directly below them. Mark's lens flashed green through the smoke and falling ash. Even at this height, Pol could feel heat upon his face.

"If I have slain your dragon, you have destroyed my shrine," Mark said softly, "just now."

With a sudden movement of his arms, he drew Nora to the edge and held her there. His lens flashed red again.

"I reject your mad offer," he stated. "If I let you go, you can acquire more supernatural assistance and attack me again one day."

"It works both ways," Pol replied. "You can rebuild again—
better, stronger. I'm willing to take that chance."

"I'm not," Mark said, twisting Nora's arm. "That rod you hold
seems to be the key to your power. Throw it down into the crater
or I'll throw her. Try using it against me now and I'll take her
along with me."

Pol looked at the rod for only a moment, then cast it out over
the edge. Mark watched it fall. Pol did not.

"Let her go," he said.

Mark pushed her back and down, so that she stumbled and fell
to the rooftop.

"Now I can face you," he said.

Pol raised his fists and moved forward.

"I am not such a fool," Mark said, sliding an oblong case from
a pocket upon his right thigh. "I remember that you've had training with your hands. Try this!"

Suddenly, Pol was able to see the roar from the nascent vol-
cano below, yellow and black-streaked, washing about him. The
rooftop buckled beneath his feet, emitting musical tones like
spikes, as the sky tipped, becoming a funnel, its terminus his
head, down which the sharp-edged clouds and swirls of smoke
were pouring. His feet were far away—perhaps in Hell—yes,
burning, and when he tried to move, he dropped to one knee and
the firmament shuddered and his eyes were moist with gems
which sliced his cheeks apart as they descended. Smooth blue
notes emerged from his mouth like escaping birds. Mark was
laughing purple rings and his orange eye was a rushing headlight.
The thing he held before him tore shimmering holes in the air,
and—

—and from one of the holes emerged seven wings of flame.

Your guitar, said the first.

Get the case off your back, said the second.

Get it out of the case, said the third.

Play it, said the fourth.

Your hands know the way, said the fifth.

Get the case, said the sixth.

Open it, said the seventh.

A black mountain flew past him, as his hands—unfamiliar things themselves—performed operations they alone understood. Blue sparks flew from three points upon the blackness. A strange and dangerous object was rising out of the shadows before him . . .

His hands made it move to his knee and began doing things they alone knew . . .

Constellations bloomed before his eyes. A throbbing began down near the place of movement . . .

Attack! said the first.

Drive back that which assails you, said the second.

Let him see as you see now, said the third.

. . . Hear as you hear, said the fourth.

You lulled the minotaur, said the fifth.

. . . This one you shall drive beyond the bounds of reason, said the sixth.

Destroy him! said the seventh.

Suddenly, he heard the music. The distortions still played about him, but he pushed them farther off. He changed the beat. He rose slowly to a standing position. The waves from the jumble-box washed over him and reality was troubled each time a portion of the broadcast broke through, reached him. But his vision cleared for longer and longer periods of time. He saw Mark, holding the box, pointing it at him, perspiration like a mask of glass upon his face. His lens was flashing wildly through the entire spectrum. He swayed. The music drowned even the rumbling below, though the smoke came and went between them. Nora knelt, head bowed, hands covering her face. Pol put more force into his strumming, driving the beat into his adversary's brain. Mark took a swaying step backward and halted. Pol advanced a step, colors swirling intermittently in the air before him. Mark retreated another pace, his lens flashing faster and faster from color to color. When the building shook again, slanting beneath their feet, Mark staggered and dropped the box. His lens went black for several pulsebeats. He put out his hands for support, took another step . . . A cloud of smoke swept over him. He fell against the parapet, and it gave way . . .

Pol stopped playing and dropped to his knees. Automatically, he lowered the guitar into its case. He began crawling toward Nora then, feeling a strong pull to his right as the building canted even more precipitously. When he reached her, he placed his hand upon her shoulder.

"I did try to save him," he said.

"I know."

She lowered her hands from her face and hugged him gently, looking away toward the rail.

"I know."

Hurry, Pol! The building is going!

He looked upward, unbelieving. A vast, dark form was sliding through the smoke.

Moonbird!

Mount as soon as I light. Only moments remaining . . .

The great dragon settled beside them, enormous open wounds upon his sides and shoulders. Pol boosted Nora onto his back, slung his guitar case and followed.

How——? Pol began.

The one called Mouseglove. I can talk with him, Moonbird said as they rose. *He lies injured at Rondoval, attended by centaurs. Your ogre destroyed all the men but the two in the ships. Fortunately, he had a weapon that slays from a distance. He says that he will be your house guest until he is whole again. He told me to come here.*

As they climbed higher, Pol summoned strands, all that he could, and clutched them for a moment.

It is over, he said. *We are going home.*

From here and there, his surviving minions rose to follow.

He looked down, once, into the raging heart of the crater.

. . . If I were to drop the seven figurines into it, he wondered, would I be free?

You are a fool, came a voice out of a sudden flame, *if you think that we—the most bound of all—are even as free as you.*

The flame faded, and Pol turned and watched the smoking mountain grow smaller as Moonbird beat his way into the sky.

I am not finished learning, he said. *But I've had enough lessons for today.*

Nora had slumped before him, but her breathing was regular. He eased her into a more comfortable position. He felt older as he regarded the sinking sun, and very tired, though he knew he could not permit himself to sleep for a long while. He reached out and touched one of Moonbird's wounds.

I am glad that someone I know won something, he said.

Later, the stars came out and he watched them all the way to home and morning.